PETER
AND THE
BLITZ

ANGELA de CAPRARIIS-SALERNO

AuthorHouse™
1663 Liberty Drive
Bloomington, IN 47403
www.authorhouse.com
Phone: 1 (800) 839-8640

Published by AuthorHouse 08/25/2017

ISBN: 978-1-5462-0508-1 (sc)
ISBN: 978-1-5462-0507-4 (e)

Library of Congress Control Number: 2017912895

Print information available on the last page.

My Mother was seventeen years old, when England
declared war against Nazi Germany.
She lived in London during the *Blitz*.
Throughout her lifetime, Mummy recounted
many of her war time experiences to me.
I dedicate this book in her memory.

My Uncle Peter was thirteen years old when
he was evacuated from London.
He continues to share these times with me.

This novel tells the story of children like him who
survived their ordeals during the *London Blitz*.

Angela de Caprariis-Salerno

Prologue

I adjusted my aviator helmet, checked the cinch on my parachute and gave the ground crew a thumb's up. The engine of my *Spitfire* purred loudly and within seconds the air craft was flying into a grey sky dotted with dark billowing clouds. I dodged between two low-flying *barrage balloons* and soared toward a dull sun.

A *Messerschmitt* suddenly appeared on my left wing. I turned my plane into a sharp right and climbed higher. The Nazi fighter plane followed me through the clouds. I turned upside down and changed course, but didn't lose him. The *Messerschmitt* was on my tail. White vapor trails from our planes crisscrossed the ominous sky.

As I dove lower, a fine mist sped past my *Spitfire* and headed toward the Nazi plane. Within seconds the enemy plane was completely engulfed in a dousing rain. A bolt of lightning hit the *Messerschmitt's* right wing and the Nazi immediately lost control of his aircraft. The plane spiraled dangerously downward. The Nazi unfastened the cockpit's window and ejected. Within seconds his parachute opened, but the pounding rain made it impossible for him to maneuver the chute. The unnerved pilot took no regard to my position immediately above him. Now was my opportunity, I steadied my plane, locked him in my sights, and---

Chapter One

"**P**eter, Peter, wake up!"

My dream was splintered!

"You must get ready, or we'll be late for church," Mum called from the bottom of the stairs.

"Five minutes more, Mum," I mumbled and snuggled deeper under the blankets.

"Oh, no you don't. You don't want to make Mum cross on such a beautiful day!"

My older sister tore off my covers and stood menacingly over me. Tillie's high heels clicked on the wooden floor as she walked to the window. Even this noise annoyed me. It was Sunday and I wanted to sleep.

"Come on, Peter. You heard Mum."

She pulled up the shade and opened the window. The morning sun raced into my room. It radiated off my sister in her bright rust colored suit. From beneath the brim of her stylish brown hat her blue eyes twinkled. She grinned widely. The dimple in her cheek became pronounced. Tillie hummed a little ditty as she left the room. My sister was perpetually happy and it was usually contagious, but today stumbling out of bed I complained.

"Can't you all go to church without me?" I shouted down the hall.

"NO!"

The Vicar's monotonous voice rambled making it very difficult for me to remain alert. I decided to count the number of times he cleared his throat when driving a point across. He had just coughed for the nineteenth time when the church doors flung open with a loud bang.

An excited parishioner pushed his way into the crowded church and shouted, **"We're at war! Prime Minister Chamberlain has declared it! We're at war with Nazi Germany!"**

We hurried home. Daddy immediately turned on the *wireless*. The news was the same. Two days ago, the Nazis had invaded Poland, and now England was going to Poland's aid. The Prime Minister told the British people he believed he had done all that one man could do to prevent a war. Chamberlain asked "God bless you all and may He defend the right…I am certain the right will prevail." It was all very exciting and at the same time very scary!

Daddy had believed war was inevitable. So, when the Anderson shelter became available for the general population by Home Secretary John Anderson, Daddy immediately ordered one for the back garden. I anxiously awaited its arrival.

One afternoon upon returning from school, Mum told me to take a look out back. Leaning against the tool shed were six tall curved panels of galvanized corrugated steel and fourteen steel panels of different sizes. Our spaniel, Toffee, had turned over a small cardboard box. Various sized nuts, bolts and washers spilled onto the ground. I reached down to pick up a large washer and realized the shelters were delivered in pieces. It was up to us to put it together.

That night I sat at the kitchen table while Daddy read the directions aloud.

"First we must dig a hole in the ground. The shelter has to be 4 feet below the earth, and stand 2 feet above the ground. The dimensions must be 4 feet deep, by 6 feet long and 4 ½ feet wide."

"George, it's going to take you quite a while to dig a hole that size," said Mum.

"No problem, Margaret. I'll have Peter help. He's a strong lad. What do you think of that idea, Peter?"

"Super, Daddy, we'll have it done in no time flat."

On Saturday, my father and I were ready to start digging, but Mum came out and put a stop to our excavation in her domain.

"Just a minute, you two! I think I should have a say as to where THIS THING is going."

Now here was a problem. There really was no clear space to dig a hole 6 feet long by 4 ½ feet wide. Every square inch of Mum's garden was taken up with flowers and vegetables. The old wooden fence on either side of the garden was covered with fragrant honeysuckle. Patches of blue iris grew next to an old wooden barrel that overflowed with thyme and rosemary. Yellow and maroon hollyhock stood tall over clumps of aromatic lavender. Hedges of delicate pink and cream roses stretched along the back of the house. Brilliant green ivy grew down a stone path twisting through the garden. Carefully arranged in perfectly straight lines, bamboo teepees supported pole beans, *marrows*, and cucumbers. Near the edges of the garden, strawberry plants and mounds of blue forget-me-nots contended for space with crisp green lettuce. At the bottom of the garden an old apple tree shaded a small wooden bench Daddy had built for Mum years ago. After completing her many chores, Mum often sat there and read with Toffee at her feet.

I understood the Anderson shelter would certainly displace much of her beloved garden. It was obvious that neither Dad nor I had a clue where to erect it without disrupting the meticulously laid out plots. Daddy gave me a wink and cleverly turned to Mum.

"Yes, Margaret, you are absolutely correct. Where should we put 'this thing'?"

Mum silently moved throughout the yard with her head tilted slightly. She was deep in conversation with herself. Toffee followed Mum while she inspected various plants. I began fidgeting. Daddy nudged me with his elbow.

"Keep still, Peter."

So, I sat on the bench and waited somewhat patiently for her decision. Finally, she gave her directions.

"George, before you dig the hole, you must remove a considerable number of flowers. When the construction of the shelter is completed, we shall replant them on top of the roof."

"What a marvelous idea! Since the shelter has to be covered with at least fifteen inches of earth this should work out perfectly."

We began our laborious chore under Mum's watchful eye. Dad did the tedious digging around the chosen plants, which I carefully removed and gave to Mum. She skillfully tied burlap around each ball of earth to hold the roots in place.

"This will protect them until they're transplanted on top of Mr. Anderson's shelter. Now, Peter, move them next to the shed for the time being."

The process took quite a while. Once completed, Dad measured the area for the foundation. He did it several times. I found this was all very tiresome and wanted to start digging. Finally, Dad pushed his shovel into the black earth and lifted out a large scoop of black earth with several fat earthworms. He pitched it all to his left and resumed digging. I picked up my shovel and matched his pace. Toffee helped by scratching up earth in all directions.

"WOO! Daddy, this is hard labor," I complained after about an hour of shoveling and pitching.

"Peter, you're doing a man's job, and you're only twelve."

That made me feel good, and I didn't stop until Mum brought lunch so we could picnic under the apple tree. Mum and Dad sat on the bench and I rested against the tree. It was a perfect spring day, birds were flying overhead, and honey bees were buzzing from one flower to another. Tiny insects investigated the mound of displaced earth. Toffee sat perfectly still watching a grey squirrel feverishly digging through the rich soil in search of any misplaced bulb to munch. I gazed at my parents.

The sun shone through the leaves lighting up Dad's face. His dark brown hair which usually was carefully combed, was plastered on his forehead. He looked relaxed after the hard work we had done. Mum peeled an apple. Her pretty face was calm. The only sounds were the whirling of lawn mowers being pushed and children's laughter several houses down the road. Everything was so peaceful. Was it really necessary to build this shelter?

"Daddy, do you think Hitler is going to attack us?" I asked.

"Yes, Peter, I am afraid he is."

"But why?" I persisted.

"Because that is his plan," my father replied. His calm face twisted as in pain.

"Come along, Peter, let's finish this hole today. Tomorrow we'll assemble the shelter."

Preparing for bed that evening, I admitted to myself that the digging had proven harder than I imagined. I was glad that part of the job was behind us. Every muscle in my body hurt. Toffee curled up into a ball at the bottom of my cot. As I slowly lowered myself onto it, she sighed deeply. I suspected even she was tired from her burrowing.

We'd never make it as ditch diggers, Toffee," I said and closed my eyes.

The next morning, Mum popped her head into my room. I had dressed in my work clothes.

"Sorry, Peter, no laboring this morning. You'll have plenty of time to do it after church."

"*Right-o,* Mum."

Although, I wished we could just start, perhaps it was for the best considering how my body ached. I quickly changed into my Sunday clothes.

We all went off to church. During the service, a visiting clergyman gave a stirring sermon asking that we sacrifice and do our part for our country in this time of war. Afterwards he prayed our military men remain safe from harm. We sang several hymns, and my off-key voice rose above the congregation when we concluded with a rousing rendition of "Onward Christian Soldiers".

Rather than linger after church and talk to friends, we hurried home. We prepared for work, and grabbed a quick bite. It was now a serious family project.

Daddy took control and gave the orders.

"Tillie, go to the left and hold that curved sheet. Margaret, stand opposite her and hold the other piece. Peter, get on the ladder inside the shelter and help hold the pieces in place. Then I'll bolt them together on top."

Frequently the metal shifted and we had to position the pieces again. This took more time than planned, but we managed to get the sides up before tea time. The six feet tall corrugated pieces of metal were embedded four feet below the ground, and the remaining two feet springing out were aligned and bolted together in the middle. The structure resembled the cover of a small bridge without a foundation.

We stood back and admired the shelter. Toffee inspected its interior. She trotted out just as a black crow landed on its roof. Protecting her domain, Toffee barked ferociously at the bird. Cawing its indignation, the crow flew off. Toffee's stubby tail wagged happily at this. When she sat down her bottom kept up the momentum. Daddy reached down and patted her silky golden head.

"What a brave dog you are, Toffee!"

"Should we start covering the top with earth?" I eagerly asked my father.

"No, that's quite enough for today. Tomorrow evening, I'll tighten all the bolts again before we do that."

"And after that's completed, you'll be able to transplant my flowers onto the top," Mum said enthusiastically.

"You'll have the most original garden in the neighborhood, Mum," Tillie laughed.

This was disappointing! I had wanted to finish the job that night. Lying in bed, I decided to surprise my father. Tomorrow immediately after school, I'd tighten the bolts. Then I'd cover the shelter with the excavated earth before Daddy came home.

I wouldn't tell anyone my idea, and the family would be proud of my achievement. The next day, my plan rushed through my mind all during school. When the dismissal bell finally rang, I waved goodbye to my friends, and ran home. I had a lot to do! Toffee greeted me with her usual rambunctious barking. Dashing into the house and up the stairs, I shouted to my mother in the kitchen.

"Hello, Mum, I've got to work on the shelter."

I tore off my school uniform and threw on my dirty work clothes.

I was down in the garden before she could question me. Nothing could stop me. I found the *spanner* my dad had used to tighten the bolts and climbed on top of the shelter. The bolts felt quite tight, so I didn't see any need to tighten them further. I slid down and started piling the earth around the shelter. *Blimey,* this was harder than digging up the earth! Toffee grabbed at my shovel. When I didn't share her game, she settled among the forget-me-nots and watched me.

I heaped the earth where the shelter protruded from the ground. Once that was done, I began dumping soil onto the roof. The earth began to slide down the sides. My arms were tired from lifting shovelfuls of earth. I didn't have the strength to pound it down with the shovel. I decided to scale onto the roof and thump the soil down with my feet.

I climbed on top, and began stomping on the earth. The soil was packing down, so I continued banging down with all my weight. I was proceeding along splendidly until I heard the sound of metal against metal, followed by several loud popping noises. Suddenly the entire roof gave way under me.

I crashed down! The curved steel sides of the shelter collapsed onto me. One of the back-metal sheets tumbled down with full force and hit me on the forehead. The earth I had piled around the shelter and onto the roof now completely buried me. Darkness engulfed me. I tried to open my mouth and shout for help, but earth filled my mouth. I spat it out and tasted blood. My legs were wedged between two heavy metal sheets and the shorter side of the hole. My right arm was pinned behind me. It was impossible to free myself! A pungent smell of damp earth filled my nostrils. This was how it felt to be buried alive! I was terrified! I heard Toffee's frantic barking. Then, somewhere far away my mother cried out my name. I tried to answer, but no sound came from my throat. My eyes lost focus. Then there was nothing.

Chapter Two

Within a month I was on a train heading north to Cumbria. Children from all over London were being evacuated. The government had declared children be sent away to safety. It was feared the Nazis would bomb London. I was lucky. Dad's sister lived in Carlisle, but the majority of children would be *billeted* with strangers. It was all very odd. Since we were tots our mums had warned us about speaking to people we didn't know. The war changed all the rules. I had boarded a train along with hundreds of children who mostly didn't know where they were heading.

An older boy was staring out the window of the compartment to which I had been assigned. His greasy black hair was flattened under a dirty cap. The grey blazer and trousers he wore were too small and quite worn.

"Hello, I'm Peter Morris," I said and stowed my bags on the overhead racks.

"Colin," the boy answered without turning from the window.

I was about to ask where he was going when a little blonde boy and girl entered. They held each other's hand and looked very frightened. A rather sour faced matron settled them in and then turned to me. She squinted at my name and destination written on the cardboard placard hanging around my neck.

"Peter Morris, is it?" she asked.

"Yes, Ma'am," I answered.

"You're going to Carlisle. These children are getting off before that. You'll watch them won't you, young man?" she said.

"Yes, Ma'am."

She hurried away without looking at the children. As soon as she left, they started crying. Colin spun around from the window. He narrowed his dark eyes. A long-jagged scar running above his left eyebrow gave him a frightening look. He pushed his blunt chin out, and shouted,

"Stop blubbering, you two."

They sobbed even harder, and I gave Colin a dirty look. I reached into my pocket and pulled out a packet of cards. I'm pretty good at handling cards. So, I did a few smart tricks. I whistled a gay tune as I played with them, and soon the boy and girl stopped crying and watched me.

"What're your names?" I asked.

"I'm Tommy and this is my sister, Alice. We're twins," the boy answered.

"Hello, Tommy and Alice. My name is Peter and that's Colin. We're going to be together for a while so why don't we have some fun while we travel along?"

Alice smiled and Tommy nodded enthusiastically. Colin said nothing. He pushed a sweet into his mouth and went back to staring out the window. I figured we weren't going to see his face for the rest of the trip. He wasn't very friendly, and the less I had to do with him the better I liked it.

"Do you know how to play rummy?" I asked the twins.

"No, would you show us?" Tommy said.

We had long pulled out of Euston Station, and were speeding along the countryside. The twins were smart and quickly picked up the game. We played for a while and they appeared happier.

Soon the rocking motion of the train lulled the twins to sleep, and before long we all nodded off. We were abruptly awoken when the train came to a loud stop and the whistle sounded. Children were ushered off the train to waiting adults on the platform. This had a terrible effect on the twins. They both started wailing uncontrollably. Nothing I did quieted them.

Colin decided to take things into his own hands. He jumped from his seat. He pushed his face into Tommy's. Then in a nasty voice he screamed.

"Why don't you two keep your *traps* shut? `Cause if you don't, I'll shut them for ye."

Colin raised his hand ready to bash Alice. I jumped up and positioned myself between him and the twins. Colin was taller and bigger than me. He had wide shoulders, and must have played rugby because his arms and legs were muscular.

"Get out of me way," he snarled.

I didn't move. This infuriated him. He threatened me.

"First I'll give ye a good thrashing and then I'll take care of them two. I'll shut them up."

The train pulled away from the station and was bouncing about again. I stood my ground. Colin stepped back. He took a wide swing and hit me in the stomach. He had quite a wallop! It left me breathless for a few seconds. Once I regained my wind, I threw myself at him and we both landed on the floor. He didn't expect this reaction from me and it was to my advantage. But Colin weighed a good *stone* more than me, and I was getting the worst of the fight.

Luckily for me the matron burst in on us. She pulled us apart.

"Boys, you will stop this immediately. What an example you are setting for these little ones. Utterly disgraceful! How very ungentlemanly!"

Throughout the scuffle the twins had been quiet. Now they came to my defense, and wanted to tell their story. They pointed at Colin.

"Ma'am, Colin wanted to 'bash' us!" Alice shouted.

"Yes, he said Peter needed a 'good thrashing' and then he 'would take care of us'. He would have done it if Peter hadn't stood up to him. He's a bully he is. He hit Peter first," Tommy added.

"Peter was like Sir Lancelot saving us," Alice told the matron.

"Like Sir Lancelot! Well, I am glad to hear there's one gentleman between you. Colin get your things and come with me," the matron said, and led Colin out.

"I'm glad he's left," Tommy said.

"Me too, he was nasty," Alice added.

They calmed down and I tried learning more about them.

"Do you have any brothers or sisters in London?"

"No, not yet. Our Mum is going to 'ave another baby. After the baby is born, she and the baby will join us. Then we'll be a family again," Alice volunteered.

"Except that Pa has to stay in London. He's a fireman, and that's an important job."

When Tommy said this, his little chest swelled with pride.

"Indeed, it is. Shall we play another game of rummy?" I asked.

We played cards again and at the next station they disembarked. Tommy and Alice had all their worldly possessions in their little cardboard *valises*. They joined a small group of evacuees who had left the train and were waiting with the authorities for people to pick them up.

The children were ready for war. Their name placards and the clumsy cardboard boxes holding the government issued gas masks hung around their necks. The boxes practically hit their knees. The matron made sure each card was clearly visible over their coats, and she kept pulling at the strings to keep things in place. Poor little tykes they looked so miserable. A young couple approached them. The woman grasped Tommy's hand and the man lifted Alice onto his shoulders. They began walking away from the station when Tommy suddenly spun around and waved goodbye. The man turned. Alice saw me at the window and blew me a kiss. I kept waving until they were out of sight.

I spent the rest of the ride by myself. I couldn't help wondering how it would be up at Auntie Nan's. I'd been there before, but always with my family. This was going to be very different.

It was still daylight and I watched the landscape change as we chugged along through towns and countryside. Everywhere the scenery looked so tranquil. It seemed impossible Britain was at war. Traveling through towns, I caught sight of posted signs warning about spies or asking for volunteers to serve on the home front. The further north we rode the signs became less frequent. Apparently, the authorities didn't think the war would reach this far north. I hoped they were right.

When the train arrived at Carlisle the sky had darkened, and the crescent moon hung high above. I recognized the tall imposing figure of my aunt standing under a platform lamp with a sheep dog at her side. Auntie Nan had turned into quite a farm woman over the years. She was dressed in a wooly red *cardigan* and a *tartan* skirt. A pair of muddy old *wellingtons* protected her feet. She even carried a tall wooden walking stick. An old tan felt hat was pulled over her thick black hair which was braided in a single plait down her back. A posy of wild flowers was tied into it. Her brilliant green eyes widened when she saw me, and she stopped talking to the elderly gentleman at her side. She called to me, and at the same time the man signaled to someone behind me. It was Colin!

Blimey! Of all the towns in England to be sent to, Colin had to go to Carlisle.

"Peter, darling, you look well. Did you have a good trip? Are you tired? Did you eat anything? Did you meet Colin on the train? This is his grandfather, Mr. White. His farm is down the hill from mine. Won't it be nice? You two boys can play together. Mr. White, you and Colin must come for tea one afternoon. Now I must hurry along. Good-bye, Colin, ta-ta, Mr. White."

Once Auntie Nan began talking it was difficult for her to stop. When there was finally a lull, I spoke up.

"It's good to see you Auntie Nan, and yes, I am a bit tired and very hungry."

We climbed aboard the donkey cart and headed for the farm situated on a highland surrounded by rolling hills, just south of the town of Carlisle. Further southwest was the Lake District, an area with nearly a hundred lakes and towering *fells* of slate and stone. The vastness of the area was amazing. I wondered how Auntie Nan, a Londoner, lived in such isolation, but of course there was the farm and its many animals.

As the cart approached the house, two barking sheep dogs ran to meet us. Their tongues lolled out of smiling mouths and their tails wagged wildly. The cart came to a stop in front of the 150-year-old house built of grey stone and mortar. When Auntie Nan opened the weathered oaken door, the dogs charged into the large farm kitchen.

A huge cast iron stove was situated on one side, and next to it under a window stood a large stone sink with a hand-pump. In the center of the room was a round antique oak table with four mismatched chairs. A cracked porcelain vase holding wild flowers and a bowl of gnarled apples sat on the table.

Off the kitchen was the parlor. Two well-stuffed upholstered chairs and a long settee had been positioned on either side of a large fireplace with a roaring fire. Over the fireplace hung a beautiful oil painting of the view from Auntie Nan's farm. My aunt was quite an artist and her artwork decorated the walls throughout her home. An easel holding a work in progress had been placed in a corner of the room next to a window. Dim lamps on two small wooden tables cast dancing shadows on the walls and floor. Opposite the windows stood a tall cupboard with a glass door containing china and treasured knick-knacks. All three dogs settled down comfortably on the worn Oriental rug covering the ancient oak floor. They raised their heads and watched as their mistress led me through the parlor.

Lugging my bags, I followed my aunt down a narrow hall with doors on either side. At the end of the hall Aunt Nan pushed open a door. The corner room had two windows on adjacent walls. Lace curtains hung from the open windows and moved gently. A chest of drawers with a picture of my dad and aunt when they were children had been placed catty-corner between the windows. A wide bed with a puffy coverlet was positioned in the center of the longest wall. Over the bed hung a watercolor of a sheep dog and a flock of sheep, another of Auntie's pieces. To the left of the bed, a small table with a low lamp and several books was conveniently nearby.

"Peter, this will be your room. It gets sun most of the day, and I'm sure you will find it comfortable. The *W.C.* is next to the kitchen, why don't you wash up and we'll have supper. I've prepared some trout I caught this morning."

Over dinner Auntie Nan told me all about life on the farm.

"Peter, things have changed since you were here years ago. I now have a working farm. There are about two dozen chickens, a rooster, five geese, several milking cows, a flock of sheep, two donkeys, three dogs, and a mother cat with her five kittens. There's a pond which is home to a family of migrating ducks. One of my neighbors gave me four rabbits, and I've begun building a hutch for them. I suspect there'll be bunnies before long."

"Aunt Nan, how do you take care of all these animals?" I asked.

"Well since your Uncle Ted joined the army, I've been doing it by myself. I get up quite early each morning. The animals must be fed. The cows milked. Eggs fetched. The sheep moved to alternate pastures. The donkeys brushed. The vegetable garden weeded. The barn mucked out. Have I left anything out?"

"I hope not, Auntie Nan. It sounds like an awful lot of work."

"Oh, Peter, it's wonderful you're here to help me out!"

I wasn't quite sure, especially when the next morning Auntie Nan woke me up at 5AM.

After a huge breakfast of eggs, *kippers*, toast and tea, Auntie Nan led me out. She handed me a pail and motioned to follow her. The farm was coming alive. The rooster flapped his wings and strutted about. The hens clucked from their coop. When Auntie Nan opened the barn door, the geese honked and waddled out. The kittens tumbled over each other hurrying into the yard. We walked into the barn and were welcomed by the cows' mooing from their stalls

"Good morning, Clover. How are you this lovely morning?"

Aunt Nan plunked down a three-legged stool and sat next to the black and white cow. Then my aunt leaned into the animal. "Now, Peter, it takes practice milking a cow. Watch how I hold her teats and squeeze them. There's a rhythm to it, and the right amount of pressure must be exerted."

Streams of milk spurted into the bucket. How difficult could this be? I asked myself, as I watched the bucket fill.

"Now you try it, Peter."

She moved to another cow. I sat on the stool and went at it. After many attempts, I finally got the knack. I was slow and only milked one cow, but Clover was very patient with me. It really wasn't so hard!

The next morning Aunt Nan asked me to milk Daffodil, an older cow she had milked the previous morning. I put my stool to the cow's left and started. Daffodil moved toward me. She kept moving closer and closer so I kept moving my stool. The cow eventually managed to squash me between the wall and her body. All the while Daffodil had been swishing her tail from side to side. I couldn't escape it. Each time it came around she whacked me full force, and turned her head. When she looked at me I swore she was laughing. This continued until I finally gave up and looked for my aunt.

"I don't understand, Auntie, cows are supposed to be gentle animals. Daffodil is torturing me. I'm trying to milk her, but she's giving me a hard time. I don't think that cow likes me."

"Nonsense, Peter, it's only because you have cold hands. Warm up your hands before you touch her."

"Warm up my hands? Right-o, I'll give it another go."

I rubbed my hands together. I blew on them. I hugged them under my armpits. I was ready. I sat on the stool, positioned the milk pail and grabbed Daffodil's teats. She snorted, and hit me so hard with her tail I fell off the stool into a pile of manure.

Aunt Nan thought this was the funniest thing she had ever seen. She laughed so hard she was unable to catch her breath and gasped for air.

"It's not funny!" I said indignantly.

"Oh yes, it is! You were bowled over by a cow. Not just any cow, but a cow named Daffodil.

Chapter Three

Dearest Jillie,

I can't believe how long I've been here! I'm sorry for not writing sooner, but I've been quite busy helping Auntie Nan on the farm. There's so much to do and she keeps telling me how glad she is I'm here. If I'm not collecting eggs or milking cows or tending sheep I'm busy feeding someone or cutting wood or hoeing the veggie garden.

Auntie Nan's animals all have unusual names. The dogs are named after mythological gods, Mercury, Zeus, and Diana. Other animals are named after flowers. The cows are Daisy, Daffodil, Clover, Rosie, and Blue Bell, Dahlia, Iris, and Lilly. The donkeys are called Jack in the Pulpit (Jack, for short) and Pansy. Even the chickens, geese, and sheep have names, but there are too many to list. The mother cat is called Her Majesty and the kittens named after historical princes and princesses. We're still thinking what to name the rabbits.

Auntie Nan spoke to the headmaster at the local school and in a few weeks, I'm going there, so I shan't be helping her as much as I've been. The school is quite a distance from the farm, but Nan has given me Uncle Ted's bicycle to use. It's a bit old but will work after I fix it up.

We went to the castle in Carlisle. Do you know about it? It was one of the castles where Mary Queen of Scots had been imprisoned. You've got to come up here and see it.

We get information about the war up here. People are calling this the "Phony War" because the Nazis haven't tried anything. Maybe nothing will happen and we evacuees can come home soon. I miss you all.

Is Toffee OK? Don't forget to brush her every day. Did any of my friends stop by? I know David and Doreen were evacuated. Did they come home?

How are Dad and Mum? Please give them my love.

It's getting late, and I must get up early tomorrow.
With all my love, your brother,
Peter

P.S.

Please tell Mum and Dad the next letter will be to them.

Chapter Four

That night a terrible storm raged without any warning. Lightning lit up the sky. Thunder rumbled loudly shaking the entire house. It woke us both up, but we didn't even have time to bring the donkeys into the barn. Auntie Nan called for the dogs, and they rushed into the house as though chased by a frightening predator. The wind roared down the *fells*. A violent steady rain pounded the roof and pelted the windows. Water leaked through the roof and onto the kitchen floor. Gusts blew through chinks in the stone, and the gas lights flickered. We sat in front of the sputtering fireplace bundled in heavy blankets. I stared into the flames and thought about the war. Everything seemed so far away. Here I was safe from it all and my family was in danger. I felt selfish. Eventually I fell asleep on the settee.

The next morning the rain stopped and the sun crept lazily across the land. After breakfast, Auntie Nan and I pulled on our *wellingtons* and went out to start our chores. The storm's damage was everywhere. Broken tree limbs hung dangerously low to the ground. Torn leaves plastered the buildings. Fallen twigs cluttered the front yard. The staked vegetable plants in the garden lay broken on the ground. Rain had poured into the barn. The chicken coop's roof had almost been torn off. Huge muddy puddles were all about.

Auntie Nan headed toward the shed where tools were stored. Over her shoulder she called to me.

"Peter, I'm going to start mending the chicken coop. But I'm particularly concerned about the sheep. Please go check on them."

"No problem, I'll go right now."

The sky had turned clear, a wind from the north swept the few remaining grey clouds across the mountains. Stately dark green pines swayed against the autumn sky. A smell of damp earth reached my nostrils and instantly triggered my memory. I recalled my accident and the terror I felt being trapped under the Anderson shelter.

At least here I didn't have to worry about the Nazis' bombs. The Nazis had dropped a few bombs over England, but the *wireless* assured the listeners they were of no importance. That selfish feeling came over me. Here I was enjoying my safety and not considering my family in London. Why was I still north? I shook my body trying to shrug the feeling off and set out to check the sheep.

I shouted for Mercury whose daughter, Diana, ran along with him. Mercury was very fast, and responded to my commands, so I felt good about this job. We went out to the pastures. After several minutes, we found the wooly creatures huddled against an ancient stone wall. Suddenly Mercury went tearing after them. A sheep tried to bolt the flock until Diana nipped at its heels. With the dogs in pursuit, the sheep ran toward me. I spun around quickly, stumbled on a root, and fell down. I really wasn't meant to be a farmer.

I was thinking this when Colin came over the hill. He appeared lost in thought, about what I wondered? I hoped he hadn't seen me. Then the way he skulked about, told me he had and was up to no good. This worried me because the sheep were skittish enough without anything out of the ordinary scaring them.

Suddenly Colin shouted my name really loud, and he hid!

"PETER! PETER!"

That's all the sheep needed. They stampeded off! The dogs ran with them, and I followed. When the sheep ran, frequently all four hooves flew off the ground, and they jumped above each other. This gave Colin the jollies. I could hear him laughing loudly from his hiding place. It took the dogs and me a while to get the flock back to the proper pasture and calmed down. I sat on a stone wall, and although it was a brisk day, I was sweating. Colin was a real nuisance and I was tempted to give him a piece of my mind. I couldn't decide if it would matter, but I remembered our battle in the train and thought better of it.

That week Auntie Nan took me to a sheep dog competition. We

brought Mercury and Zeus, her lead sheep dog with us. Farmers brought their sheep dogs from all around to compete to see which dog was the best at herding sheep. The farmers whistled and called different sounds, and the dogs took their lead from those noises. The whole contest was based on time and agility. It was fascinating to watch how the dogs cornered the sheep, blocked them, and eventually corralled them into the pen.

Auntie Nan was the only woman entered in the competition. When it was her turn she flung her long plaid cloak onto the ground, and boldly sauntered into the ring with Mercury following her. With her tall walking stick, Auntie Nan pointed to the sheep. Mercury immediately bounded toward the animals. My aunt whistled and called to Mercury who circled them. One sheep broke loose. Auntie signaled to the dog that instinctively cornered the animal and forced it back to the others. Then Mercury herded them all into the pen.

A low rumble of approval came from the farmers. But the day was not over. Auntie Nan remained in the arena. She motioned to Mercury, and the dog trotted to me where he sat.

Then my aunt whistled and Zeus ran to her side. The sheep were let out. Zeus flew after them. Auntie commanded softly.

He took direction, and with his head to the ground, tightly herded them together. Auntie Nan whistled, and within seconds Zeus drove them all in the pen. The dog had accomplished this feat in record time.

A roar of admiration rose from the men. My aunt smiled, gave Zeus a hug and calmly left the circle. We waited for the results. Auntie Nan won first place with Zeus and second place with Mercury!

"Well done, Auntie!"

"Peter, let's celebrate. I think I'll invite Mr. White and his grandson to tea. It will be nice for you to talk with a boy from London. What do you think?"

Indeed! What did I think? I hadn't told her what happened in the train, or what was happening on the farm. If I did, maybe she wouldn't invite them, but I said nothing. That evening Colin and I had tea under the same roof, and behaved like perfect gentlemen. My aunt was busy talking to Mr. White when she politely addressed Colin.

"Colin, your granddad tells me your father is stationed in Gibraltar, just like my husband, Teddy."

Colin barely nodded and continued munching on a *scone.* Since he didn't offer anything to the conversation my aunt turned her attention back to his grandfather.

Mr. White reached for another cucumber sandwich, gulped it down and then responded to my aunt's statement.

"Yes, he was one of the lucky ones evacuated from *Dunkirk.* Stayed here for a while, then was sent to Gibraltar. Colin's mum is a shop girl in *Selfridge's.* He was home by himself most o' the day, so I 'ad her send Colin north to spend time with me on the farm."

"What a wise decision, Mr. White." Aunt Nan smiled.

Colin remained silent and sucked on a sweet he produced from his pocket. Once or twice I caught him staring at me.

After they left, Auntie Nan approached me.

"Peter, that boy, Colin, appears to be very troubled. And that scar on his head. I wonder what his home life was like in London?"

Was Auntie Nan asking me a question, or telling me something? That night lying in bed I kept thinking about what she had said. What was his home life like in London?

"Peter, I'd like you to check on the ducks. I've been told there's a fox in the area. I'm afraid he may have gotten to them." Auntie Nan was sitting at the kitchen table mending an old skirt when she had this idea.

"Right-o!"

"Be careful at the pond's edge. It probably is quite slippery after that storm."

I wrapped a woolen scarf around my neck and hurried out to the pond. It was midday and the sun shone brightly overhead. The hours of sunlight were getting shorter, so I enjoyed every bit of sun. I whistled to Mercury and together we searched for the ducks.

Most of the time they were either in the pond or resting around it, but this particular day they were nowhere to be seen. The wind had uprooted an old willow tree. It had fallen onto the far side of the pond where I heard quacking. I cautiously made my way along the pond's edge toward the noise.

"HOOLA! HOOLA!" Someone shouted from behind a tree.

The ducks took off in one huge swoop. They skimmed the surface of the pond and headed toward me. My feet slipped on the slimy edge. I grabbed for a branch of the fallen tree. I missed it and dropped into the water. As I hit the pond, loud laughter resonated throughout the hills. It was Colin!

I was covered with muck from head to toe. By the time I walked the mile home I was shivering with cold.

"Peter, whatever happened to you?" Auntie Nan asked.

"I fell into the pond!"

She had a hard time not laughing, and wisely decided not to remind me she had warned me. Instead she was consoling.

"I'll heat some water for you to take a warm bath. After that, we'll have tea and you go straight to bed. I'm afraid you might get a chill."

That was exactly what happened. For the next few days I was laid up with chills and a wicked cough. Auntie Nan was a great nurse. She brought me hot soup and tea, and made sure I was comfortable. But I was miserable. I wanted to be home.

Chapter Five

Saturday was market day. After I hitched Pansy to the cart, Auntie Nan and I clogged along to town. We left the cart in a protected spot and settled on a time to meet.

Although I enjoyed market days, I dreaded meeting Colin who often accompanied his grandfather. But today I was thrilled to see that Mr. White was alone, so I casually meandered about the village. I took my time looking at the livestock and listening to the farmers praising their animals. I strolled through the food stalls and after sampling several tarts I bought two for Auntie Nan and me to share at tea time. Then I wandered over to the second-hand book stand, my favorite booth. Here I spent a lot of time leafing through the worn books and quickly lost all sense of time until the church bell rang twice.

I was late! It was time to meet Auntie Nan. I dashed to where we had left Pansy. But I couldn't find the donkey or the cart. I ran up and down the narrow streets. Frantically I searched for over an hour. Then far from the market, on the other side of town I found them. I had no idea how they had gotten there until I saw a familiar *sweet* wrapper stuck on a wheel. COLIN!

"Peter, where have you been? You were supposed to have met me here an hour ago?" Auntie Nan asked angrily as I approached her.

"I'm sorry Aunt Nan. I forgot where I left Pansy and the cart."

How I wanted to get even with Colin. He was a bully, and I was a little afraid of him. He was making my stay on the farm unbearable. I wished I was back in London far away from him.

It was Sunday morning. I didn't have to go to school, but the chores still had to be done. I lumbered out of bed and sleepily walked into the kitchen. Unlike other mornings, the room was ablaze with light. A white coconut cake with thirteen candles sat in the center of the table. Several brightly wrapped packages and envelopes surrounded the large cake. I'd been so worried about Colin and his pranks that I had forgotten my birthday.

"Happy Birthday, Peter!" Auntie Nan shouted and threw her arms around me.

"What a fabulous surprise!" I stammered.

"Sit down, dear. I'll pour us a cup of tea and we'll have cake for breakfast. But first you must blow out the candles. Make a wish. Your mother told me coconut is your favorite."

"Auntie Nan, how'd you manage to get a coconut with the war and rationing."

"I wrote your Uncle Ted if it was possible to get a coconut in Gibraltar. I've no idea how he did. He sent it with a note for you among the cards."

I blew out the candles with one great breath. Then I cut two huge slices of cake for both of us. It was delicious! I hadn't eaten coconut in such a long time and it was a real treat. After I finished my second piece of cake, I grabbed the largest package.

"That one is from your parents, Peter."

"A new pull-over. How nice."

I hoped my disappointment wasn't too obvious. I had wished I'd be getting a pair of long trousers for my thirteenth birthday. I read their card.

Dearest Peter,

We hope you like this pull-over. The green color is all the rage now. We anxiously look forward to the day when we see you again. We miss you very much.
Have a very Happy Birthday with Auntie Nan.

Hugs and Kisses,
Mummy and Daddy

Tillie sent me a copy of the latest Edgar Wallace mystery with a note.

> *Darling Peter,*
>
> *You can now start reading grown-up books. You're thirteen! I read it and it's really quite exciting.*
> *Happy Birthday, Love Tillie*

Auntie Nan had knitted me a blue and green scarf which she wrapped around a box of chocolate covered almonds. I dared not ask how she acquired those, but I suspected the black market existed even in Carlisle. On a tiny card with a drawing of a sheep she wrote:

> *To my dear Peter,*
>
> *It's wonderful having you here, I hope you will always remember this birthday.*
>
> *With all my love, Auntie Nan*

Uncle Ted's note read:

> *Dearest Peter,*
>
> *I'm sorry I can't be with you to enjoy your coconut cake. It took a lot of bargaining with the locals to procure the most important ingredient. I hope it was worth it!*
>
> *Have a very happy birthday. Love, Your Uncle Ted.*

A large envelope with a card and a *P* embossed handkerchief was from Doe.

Hello Peter,

HAPPY 13th BIRTHDAY!!

Did you think I'd forget? Mum didn't even have to remind me! I guess everyone is writing they miss you. Well I do too! It's not the same without you and David around.

You can see from the postmark that I'm in London. Since nothing seemed to be happening for the past months, Mum and Dad had us return home. At school children are slowly coming back. There was talk they were going to combine some classes, but now that the evacuees are coming back who knows?

I sent David a letter which he's supposed to forward on to you with his information included. Once you read it, you are to add your bit and send it off to me just as I wrote in the letter. We'll keep letters circulating like this and stay in touch. I'm sure it's still on David's dresser! Did you get it?

Daddy said he doesn't think the Nazis will use poisonous gas as they did in WWI. Maybe we won't have to carry these absurd boxes with the masks. My youngest sister painted hers lilac. I wonder what the ARPs will say about that?

Have a wonderful birthday, hope to hear from you soon. Cheerio, Dee

The last small envelope contained a pencil drawing of a birthday cake with thirteen candles and a short letter from David.

Happy Birthday, Peter

How're you doing? I'm O.K. Nothing exciting here.

The folks who I've been sent to are nice, but old. I'm getting pretty good playing whist.

Take care, David

P.S. Do you ~~rembring~~ remember agreeing to forwarding letters? Where does Doe get these ideas? Blimey she can write!

I read all the letters again. How lucky Doe was being home in London. I was envious. Even though David didn't sound so happy about the letter business, I thought it was a good idea and hoped he would send it off soon.

Once our chores were completed we hurried off to church. We bundled up and this time I hitched Jack to the cart. Auntie Nan had another surprise.

"Peter, I've decided it's such a special day, we should have a picnic. I packed a hamper and after church we'll make for a little lake nearby where we can have lunch."

We spent the rest of the afternoon walking around the lake. Most of the leaves had fallen off the trees, and they looked so stark against the grey hills. I wondered if the apple tree in our garden back home had lost its leaves and the apples picked. Auntie Nan broke my thoughts.

"Tomorrow you're to begin school. Are you excited, Peter?"

I nodded. Secretly I dreaded the idea of meeting up with Colin at the school.

"Auntie Nan, do you think Colin will be in my class?"

"No, as a matter of fact he won't be attending school at all. The chap who works on Mr. White's farm signed up with the RAF. Mr. White needs Colin to help him."

This was great news, but I couldn't show it.

"I wonder if Colin is happy with that arrangement."

"For some reason, I suspect he might be. Come along, Peter, I want to show you a pretty waterfall."

A couple of weeks later, the landscape changed overnight. A snowstorm howled over the *fells* and across the lakes. The winds blew east, and snow covered the neighboring hills. Tall evergreens were weighed down with ice. Snow drifted along the roads and paths. The air was frigid. Each morning additional icicles hung from the house, and the sun sparkled on the snow-covered roofs. The hours of daylight shortened, and night came upon us quickly.

After the first snowfall we housed the donkeys, sheep and cows in the barn with the cats and geese. We moved the chickens and rabbits into a smaller building, and the dogs came into the house. The animals were all comfortable and warm and didn't seem to mind the new arrangements. Mercury had taken to sleeping with me at night the way Toffee did at home. I enjoyed his company, and felt a little guilty about this when I thought about my Toffee.

There would be no snow today. The moon was still visible, and the sun was slowly coming over the horizon ready to compete for its place in the sky. The air was crisp and dry. I kept my head down against an Arctic wind and pedaled to school. I had met a few children from London, and we traded our experiences away from home. Some of them were being treated worse than Oliver Twist and wrote home begging to return to London. Others complained about having to share their room with several children. One child showed us a dark purple bruise on his arm, and quickly covered it up when a large dark-haired girl shouted at him to get into the school.

As I listened to their stories, I realized how very lucky I was to be with Auntie Nan. She really liked having me with her and it was even fun being on the farm. Truly the only problem I had in Carlisle was Colin, or was I fooling myself? That guilty nagging feeling kept bothering me. Up north I was safe from the Nazis, while my family remained in London. Was this right?

Chapter Six

The house smelled of cinnamon, cloves, ginger, nutmeg and peppermint. The larder was stocked with mince pies and puddings and *biscuits*. For a *fortnight* Auntie Nan had been spending hours baking in preparation for Christmas.

It was Christmas Eve and school was on holiday. I had finished cleaning the lunch things, when I heard Auntie Nan calling from outside.

"Peter, Peter, are you there?"

She banged open the front door, and pulled in a small snow-covered pine tree.

"Good show, give me a hand here, Peter."

Auntie Nan removed her mittens and wool hat and shrugged out of her long coat. She dropped to the floor and pulled off her boots while the two dogs tugged at the scarf hanging from her neck.

"What's this?" I said and pointed to the evergreen.

"It's a Christmas tree, you ninny. Now help me get it into the parlor and set up. I have decorations somewhere. We've got to have everything ready before they come."

"Before who comes?" I asked.

"Oh, didn't I tell you? Must've slipped my mind. Your mum, dad and sister are coming today to spend the holidays with us. I believe they're even bringing Toffee."

"Auntie Nan, what a surprise!"

"I thought you'd think so."

I nailed two pieces of wood to the bottom of the tree trunk while my aunt filled a large basin with water in which to stand the tree. Then she rummaged through a cupboard searching for the ornaments.

Soon the floor was covered with delicate glass balls wrapped in yellowing tissue paper. A set of cardboard orchestra instruments including violins, drums, harps, and trumpets tumbled from an ancient paper box. Strings of tiny red and gold glass beads were carefully removed from their cotton wool. Then Auntie Nan gently unwound yards of cheese cloth to uncover an angel dressed in white lace with golden wings.

"Peter, you may place her on the top of the tree. Be careful with her, she's quite old. Belonged to my mother when I was your age."

This was very special! I carefully reached up high and attached the angel. We began decorating the tree. Once finished, I stepped back to admire our work.

"What a beautiful tree, Auntie Nan! Thank you."

Outside, the snow had stopped falling and the air was quiet. In the distance, a dog barked and bells jingled. Zeus raised his head and Diana whined. Mercury continued sleeping. The dog's barking grew louder. I looked out the window. A horse drawn sleigh came up the hill.

"Auntie Nan, they're here!"

I ran out to greet my family.

Toffee jumped from Tillie's lap and dashed to me. I caught her in my arms. She licked my face and squirmed happily in my embrace.

"Toffee, my good girl. It's so wonderful to see you. Come meet your cousins."

Auntie Nan's three dogs that bounded out of the house with the excitement, and circled Toffee. After a certain amount of sniffing the dogs calmed down, and obviously Toffee was accepted into the pack.

"Peter, dear. You've grown!"

Mum embraced me tightly, her pretty face rosy from the chill air. She resembled a little girl with a woolen cap tightly hugging her head and loose curls peeking out.

Next, Dad grabbed me and messed up my hair. He laughed heartily as he did this.

"Have you forgotten what a barber is? Your hair is over your ears."

Then Tillie pulled me to her and whispered into my ear.

"You look quite the lad, my farmer-brother."

During all this I didn't have a chance to talk. It was grand being surrounded by them. I picked up their *valises* and parcels and easily carried them into the house.

"My, you have grown. You've gotten muscles under that pullover," Dad said.

"Life on the farm must have something to do with it, Daddy," Tillie joked.

They were right, and I hadn't even realized it.

Soon coats, gloves and hats were removed. Everyone was talking and laughing at once. The dogs sniffed each other and then nestled in front of the fire. Auntie Nan put tea up, while Mum and Tillie set the table. Suddenly the house felt like home. This was going to be a wonderful Christmas!

Church bells pealed loudly announcing that Christmas day had arrived, but eggs had to be collected, cows milked, and the animals fed. Auntie Nan and I did the milking while Mum and Tillie fed the animals. Dad hitched Jack and Pansy to the larger cart, and soon we clambered aboard heading for church.

Inside I realized that even if my eyes were blindfolded, I would have known the church was full of farmers and their families. The church smelt of damp wool, hay and dogs. We raised our voices and sang several carols. When it was time for the homily the vicar reminded us that his son was in the navy somewhere in the Atlantic. He told us he knew how people felt to have loved ones away at war, and prayed for all of them. Auntie Nan's eyes watered. I thought of Uncle Ted, and prayed he would return safely home to her. Many people sniffled, and I suspected the vicar had touched the folks in the church. I wondered how our servicemen were celebrating Christmas.

Upon our return home, I inspected the gifts under the tree. I found the wrapped gifts I had asked Auntie Nan over a month ago to send to London.

"Auntie Nan, you didn't post my gifts!"

"Of course, I didn't. Why should I waste money on postage, when everyone would be here for Christmas?"

My family had kept this secret from me for a long time. I wondered if they had done it for fun, or because they weren't sure how the war might change things. How many children were celebrating Christmas without their families? That nagging feeling tugged at me again.

"Here you go, Peter, open your gift."

Mum handed me a large package wrapped in colorful paper.

"Try not to tear the paper, Peter, I may need it for next year. If this war keeps up I doubt I'll be able to get any holiday wrappings." Auntie Nan said this as she passed Dad a cup of tea and a warm *scone* with raspberry preserves.

"A pair of long trousers! Oh, thank you Mum and Dad."

"Open my gift now, Peter," Tillie said and handed me a small box with a red ribbon around it.

Inside was a brown leather belt. "Tillie, this is perfect."

Auntie Nan had knitted me a blue and red striped woolen cap and matching mittens. I immediately stuck the cap on my head and pulled on the mittens.

"Absolutely stunning," Tillie laughed.

Mum loved the wooden jewelry box I had built from bits of pine bark I had collected. Tillie oohed and aahed over the photo album I had made of old pieces of cardboard I had found and decorated. Dad was genuinely pleased with the little leather pouch I had sewed for his tobacco.

But when Auntie Nan opened her present I knew I had given her the right gift.

"Peter, Oh my! This is absolutely beautiful. What a dear boy you are."

"It's for when you enter competitions, Auntie Nan. Several weeks before Christmas, I found this perfect maple branch. At night when you were asleep, I stained and polished it."

I was very pleased with myself!

Christmas dinner was enormous! There were carrots, and Brussel sprouts, potatoes and turnips, turkey and stuffing and a Christmas pudding. After supper, we played *Put and Take* until it was late and we all shuffled off to bed.

Mum and Dad slept in the room next to mine. I listened to their whisperings. From the parlor Tillie hummed softly as she brushed her hair one hundred times. Suddenly I realized how much I missed those sounds, and although my family was with me I grew homesick.

On *Boxing Day* Auntie invited Mr. White and Colin for tea. Mr. White arrived with a basket of dried plums and apples. The adults chatted about the war while Colin and I looked through the old newspapers Dad brought up to Carlisle for me. Finally, they left. Once again Colin had been under the same roof with me. We had hardly spoken, and he even looked sad. I remembered Auntie Nan's words: 'what was his home life like?' That night, I went to bed knowing the next day my parents and sister would be returning to London, and leave me safe in Carlisle. What a coward I was.

When they left, each day was like the last, dark and cold, and sometimes lonely. After what seemed like forever, the days slowly grew longer. The ice and snow melted. The heather bloomed and the hills turned mauve. Tiny buds of yellow, purple, and white blossomed across the green land, and trees sprouted buds. The ducks flew back from their winter quarters, and the cows were let out to pasture. The dogs ran in the fields herding the sheep. Lambs were born. The countryside was alive again, and so was Colin.

He continued to menace me. If he wasn't tripping me up with my arms full of packages on market day, he was pestering me in the pastures with the animals. I was growing weary of his pranks. There were other boys in the area, but Colin had nothing to do with them. He moped around the town and only perked up when I appeared. I didn't understand it.

Each night, Auntie and I listened to the *wireless* for news of London. As the weeks went by it appeared the war everyone predicted was never going to happen. War progressed on the Continent, and I waited for the Nazis to begin their invasion of England. Once every so often a stray bomber flew over Great Britain, and dropped a few bombs, but it was not what anyone had been expecting.

I wrote to my parents and begged to come home, considering the enemy was not invading England. I told them that I was terribly unhappy and could not adjust to the country. I wrote that since they left, I had trouble sleeping and even had difficulty concentrating at school. I was quite melodramatic in my description of my pathetic life away from London.

It worked, and when spring was in full bloom I was home. The Phony War continued through the summer. Life was almost normal.

Chapter Seven

On September 7, 1940, the *Blitzkrieg* of London began.

"What's happening? What's that?"

I rolled over in my bed when I heard the sirens. I was now awoken and living the nightmare we had been experiencing for the past few days. Hitler's *Luftwaffe* was heading toward London, and the *Heinkel III* bombers would soon be shelling the city. I quickly stretched my legs off the bed. My bare feet hit the cold floor. I grabbed my robe and gas mask. I pushed one foot into a shoe, dropped to my knees and looked under the bed for the other one.

Daddy ran into my room.

"Hurry, Peter. Mum and your sister are down in the shelter. We must get down there now!"

Daddy's icy hand tightly gripped my arm. He pulled me up and led me toward the stairs. I hobbled on one shoe, and together we made our way through the dark house. The sirens screamed into the night. I heard what sounded like distant thunder. The raid had begun.

We rushed out the back door and into the garden. London was dark. The *Air Raid Precaution Wardens* had done their job. All the houses and street lights had been extinguished. I could not make out any details of the neighboring houses. In the dark, they all resembled huge ant hills. Our garden was in shadows, and I could barely see the Anderson shelter I had helped my father build behind the house. It seemed like such a long time ago.

My recollection was interrupted by the ferocious night sounds. Sirens blared, aircraft engines roared, bombs whooshed down, anti-aircraft artillery discharged, and explosions rumbled in the distance.

Couldn't I stay in the house? Did I have to follow everyone into the shelter?

Mummy was waiting at the entrance. When she saw me hesitate she rushed to my side.

"It will be all right, Peter. Don't stop. The planes are over the East End already."

She gently pushed me into the shelter. Daddy followed and pulled the heavy canvas across the opening. He had thought of attaching a wooden door, but the warden had advised him against it. If there was a direct hit nearby, the wooden door might shatter and send splinters into the shelter and into us.

He had considered running electricity from the house, but thought better about it since the shelter was all steel and could conduct electricity should something hit the live wires. The only light in the shelter came from a small battery powered *torch* that Mum was holding. Dad had laid wooden planks on the ground as flooring, and then covered them with *lino*. He hoped this would prevent the floor from being too damp. He had placed two benches on either side of the shelter, and had tried to make the interior jolly by painting the steel walls yellow.

Tillie had painted windows on the corrugated steel to give the effect of looking out on a green pasture. This was a pretty clever feat since the steel was not flat but rather curvy. Regardless of all these attempts it still was a terribly frightful place for me.

At the far end was a small wooden table covered with a cheerful *oil cloth*. On top of that were four chipped tea cups and a wooden bowl containing several apples from our tree. A straw basket had been placed on the table. Mum kept the basket ever ready at the kitchen door. It held a tin of *biscuits* and a thermos of tea she prepared daily just in case we needed to take cover. When the alarms sounded, the first person out the back door was responsible for bringing the basket to the shelter.

Under the table was a bin with a pack of playing cards, several board games including my favorite, *Snakes and Ladders*, and an assortment of old magazines. We had tried playing cards one night, but the bombs shook us so much we stopped in the middle of a game. Stored beneath one bench was a covered bucket should we need it for *necessities*, as Mum delicately put it. So far, I hadn't needed to use the bucket. Under the second bench Dad had a crate containing various tools which he had said might be useful in the event of an emergency. I didn't want to think what type of emergency he meant.

Near the entrance stood a gallon metal milk can filled with water. Every day Tillie was responsible for changing the water so that we would have fresh water available in the night should a raid occur. The first time we spent the night in the shelter, I had asked for a cup of water. Although it was clean water I imagined it smelled of earth and found myself reliving my accident. I had never asked for water again while in the shelter, even when I was dying of thirst.

Being tall for my age, my head narrowly missed the ceiling. I bent down and moved toward my sister. My eyes were glassy from having been awoken so abruptly. I ran my fingers through my hair, and opened my mouth in a wide yawn. The stench of damp earth filled my nostrils. The night chill caused me to shiver so I pulled my robe around me, but the thin flannel didn't protect me. My feet were cold, especially the bare one. My sister looked up at me. I could see Tillie's wide grin and her blue eyes dance even in the darkness. She held Toffee tightly in her arms because the poor animal was shaking uncontrollably. I gave Tillie what I thought was a brave smile.

"Tillie, mind if I snuggle up with you and Toffee? Daddy rushed me out so quickly I didn't have time to dress properly."

"Come over here you baby," she playfully answered.

She tugged at the wool blanket she had stripped from her bed and made room for me. Mum didn't want to store blankets in the shelter because they would get moldy, so we were to bring our blankets down. Naturally I usually forgot mine. Tillie didn't mind sharing her cover with Toffee and me. She really was a grand sister.

Tillie worked for a dress designer in the West End of London. On several occasions, the raids began before she reached home, and she ended up finding protection in the *Underground* along with her friends. For my sister, this was an adventure. After the all-clear sirens sounded, Tillie hurried home. Usually her brown hair was messed, and her clothes dirty from spending the night on the filthy floor. That didn't stop her from immediately telling us stories about the sights she had seen. She was a great story teller, and would have me eagerly listening while she relayed her tale. Some of them were frightful experiences. She was the bravest girl I know.

Arranging my long body on the bench I used my sister's shoulder as a pillow, and Toffee nestled into me. Even though Tillie tried to make me comfortable I knew it was impossible for me to fall asleep. The walls of the shelter shut in on me. The sounds above were too near. The smell of earth nauseated me. I heard the whooshing of a bomb as it descended to the ground, then a powerful explosion. My body tensed, Toffee shuddered, and Tillie pulled me nearer, but it did not comfort me.

I fearfully wondered whether the shelter could withstand the shocks of the nearby explosions? Would we be directly hit? Would I survive the night? Would poor old Toffee be able to calm down?

The ground about us shook and earth fell through the cracks of the shelter. In the soft light, I saw my Mum and heard her quiet prayers. I barely made out Dad's shadow, he never moved. I wished I had a bit of his courage. I needed my fears dispelled.

"Daddy, we'll be all right, won't we?" I whispered.

"Of course, Peter. No need to worry," he answered.

"But it did fall down once."

I was remembering my terrifying catastrophe.

"Yes, but after that we built our shelter quite strong,"

His words were meant to be comforting, but they didn't erase the memory of my accident over a year ago. I tried unsuccessfully to sleep.

I heard Tillie's heavy breathing, and opened my eyes. She had managed to fall asleep despite the unbelievable noises around us. She had wrapped the blanket around Toffee's head. It muffled the noises, so even the little dog was dozing. I could hear Mum and Dad speaking softly to each other. I was the subject of their whispers.

"Margaret, we made a terrible mistake. Peter should have stayed with Nan," Daddy said with great conviction.

"George, we had no idea it would be like this. Who knew what the Nazis had planned?" Mum answered.

"I don't understand why he didn't like being with Nan. She's a softie, especially when it comes to children. The farm has just the right amount of animals to tend to. It isn't hard work. There are plenty of youngsters his age in the area. He should have had a fabulous time."

"Maybe it had nothing to do with her, or with the farm. Perhaps it concerned the school up there," my mother suggested.

Mum turned the small *torch* toward me to see if I was sleeping. I quickly shut my eyes and breathed steadily. She assumed I was sleeping, and they continued talking.

"Now that I look back on it, I wonder if his complaints about school were warranted," Daddy said.

My hearing was quite sharp so regardless of the sounds overhead, I caught most of their discussion. Dad blamed himself for putting me in jeopardy now that the Nazis had begun bombing London. Mummy tried desperately to console him, but nothing she said made any difference. His decision was made. As soon as possible, I was to be sent back north away from Hitler's *Blitzkrieg*. In the dim light of her *torch*, Mum nodded her head in agreement. My fate had been decided, and I had no say in the matter.

My thoughts whirled about in my head. Forced into the shelter each night, all I thought about was the total darkness that had overcome me when it collapsed. I argued facts to myself. Maybe returning to the north was not such a bad idea. But I'd be a coward to leave my family again. Besides, I didn't have the fabulous time my father talked about. There was Colin.

The bombing did not let up. It must have been nearing morning when I heard the all too familiar sound of a *Heinkel III* bomber overhead and the whooshing of multiple bombs being dropped. Very nearby, the bombs hit their target with such force that the entire shelter seemed to rise off the ground. I fell off the bench with a loud thud. Tillie was awoken and let out an unexpected wild scream. Toffee started barking. Mum and Dad had been deep in conversation when the explosions occurred. Mum fell to her knees, and Dad bent down to help her. Toffee jumped down and hid between the bin and the wall. Apples rolled on the floor in water spilled from the container. Tea cups were smashed when the thermos toppled over them. I coaxed Toffee from her hiding place and held her tightly to my chest. Her whole body trembled in fear. I knew how she felt.

"Tillie, Peter, are you both okay?" my father shouted above the din of the explosions.

"Yes, Dad, we're fine, but poor old Toffee is shaking something terrible."

He reached out for me. With Toffee in tow, I sat next to him. I tied the bottom ends of my robe over the poor dog's ears. Mum scooted next to Tillie. We held onto each other to ease our fear. The Nazis were sending wave upon wave of their bombers and escort fighters. Hitler was determined to bring London to her knees. He was ruthless.

We were all very quiet. Then in her light-hearted manner, Tillie asked us.

"Did I ever tell you about the rabbit and the air raid?"

Such a strange question distracted all of us.

"No," Daddy said.

Even in the dim light I could see Tillie's face transform. She tossed her thick brown hair about her shoulders. Her eyebrows arched up and her blue eyes grew wider. Her lips pursed into a devilish smile. Her voice took on a breathy quality. Tillie began reliving the experience.

"Well, this happened a few months ago, while most of the theatres were still open, and bombing was very sporadic. When the air raids sounded, all action on the stage immediately stopped. Audiences were forced to leave a play and find shelter often at the most inopportune times. Perhaps a murder was about to be solved, or maybe a magician had begun sawing a lady in half. Quite a nuisance! Nevertheless, the theater-goers had to find shelter and the most logical place for them was in the Underground. This particular night several of us had been working late when the sirens began. We quickly locked up the shop, and made our way for the nearest Underground, which was Tottenham Court Station.

The city lights had already been turned off and it was very dark. We held each other's hands and made a mad dash to the station. That day I foolishly had decided to wear my high heels and was having quite a bit of difficulty running in them. I removed them and ran through the streets in my bare feet. Along the way I stepped on some horribly squishy things, and didn't want to guess what they might have been."

"That sounds quite disgusting, Tillie," I said.

"Yes, it was. Trust me I will never do that again."

"What happened next?" Mum asked.

"When we arrived at Tottenham Court there were ever so many people pushing to get down the stairs and onto the platform below. A warden tried desperately to control the crowd, but didn't succeed. He was swept away with all of us and found himself at the bottom of the stairs. Poor old boy tried to climb back up, but after two attempts he turned around and gave up.

He followed our group and found a little corner where he settled in. He sat quite still for several minutes. Then he pulled a much-used harmonica from his coat pocket. For the longest time, all he did was rub it against the palm of his hand until finally he began playing. Although he played rather well, the tune was so melancholic that when he began to play it again, a rather large woman complained.

'Ay, we ain't at a funeral yet, pal. How about playing something a bit cheery for us who intend to see the light of day?'

This got all us girls laughing, and we began making some jolly requests of the man who eagerly obliged. I was so busy singing that I didn't notice the platform was getting very crowded. The throngs of theatre-goers were seeking shelter. Just a few minutes earlier these people had been enjoying a professional theatre troupe in a glamorous theatre. Now they were being entertained by an entirely different performance in a damp and smelly cavernous hole. Many appeared unconcerned with their surroundings and joined us in song. Others moved away seeking a quieter spot deeper in the tunnel, away from our melodies. I suspect they did not appreciate our repertoire."

Tillie raised her voice a couple of octaves and began singing *Knees Up Mother Brown*, a Cockney song dating back to World War I which was gaining in popularity again "Tillie, you are a great story teller, but not a great singer," Daddy laughed.

"Right-o! Well anyway, we were busy singing when an extremely elegant gentleman wearing a top hat and evening cloak arrived on the platform. He looked dreadfully out of place, and I wondered if he felt conspicuous.

He was tall and slender and had very fine features. His nose was long and thin and his dark grey eyes were shaded by thick dark lashes. His lips were set in a slight grin, as though he was enjoying yet another show. He had a square chin marred by a very small scar that gave him a very appealing look. His wavy black hair was combed back from his face. Yes, he was quite appealing."

"You managed to see all this in the gloomy light of the Underground?" I asked her.

"Yes!"

"What were you doing, sitting on top of him in your bare feet?"

"No, silly, but when I first saw him, I quietly suggested to my friends that we should get a little nearer to him. They agreed and we did. My friends and I could not take our eyes off him. He slowly stripped the kid gloves from his hands and tucked them neatly away in a hidden pocket inside his cloak. This accomplished, he undid the clasp at his neck. Then with a grand flourish, he removed the cloak from his shoulders. He was attired in full evening dress. He wore black tails, a pristine white shirt, white bow tie, and a black satin vest adorned with a gold watch and chain. His trousers' legs had perfect razor-sharp creases front and back, with a satin stripe running down each side. This man was definitely not in his element.

I whispered to my friends, 'Poor chap, I suspect he probably wishes he was a thousand miles away from all of this.'

It was terrible how we scrutinized him, and even our little musician stopped playing and stared at him. All walks of life find safety in the Underground during the attacks. This man was so regal in the belly of London that I marveled at his manner and temporarily forgot why I was in the bowels of the city. I found myself fanaticizing, and wondering who he might be? What had he been doing? Where was he going?

As though he knew I was thinking about him, he slyly looked up and nodded. I lowered my head ever so slightly and coyly smiled back.

My friends saw this exchange and giggled like silly school girls. His grin widened, and I had the impression he was enjoying the attention."

"Tillie, you are something! Even an air raid doesn't stop you from flirting!" Mum laughed.

"I wasn't flirting! I was being friendly. Anyway, the minutes ticked away and he casually leaned against the grimy wall. All the while he continued stroking the brim of his top hat.

Resting near him was a mother and her two children. The smaller of the two, a little boy, moved away from her and boldly walked up to the gentleman. The child stood directly in front of the gentleman, looked him up and down, and in a very London accent questioned him.

'Sir, are ya a magician?'

You can imagine how, considering his appearance and demeanor, those of us nearby reacted. There was a collective gasp. The man shook his head and laughed jovially. Then in a deep resonant voice, which I shall never forget, he answered.

'No, child. I most certainly am not a magician.'

The little boy was visibly disappointed, but did not walk away. He pulled a tattered old toy rabbit from under his jacket. He pointed to the man's top hat.

'Well sir, I was hoping ya was. Cause then me bunny would'a ad a safe place ta hide.'

The gentleman looked down at the boy and his stuffed rabbit. The man's dark eyes sparkled and his mouth broke into a dazzling smile.

'My young man, your bunny shall most definitely have a safe place to hide.'

Then to everyone's amazement, he tousled the boy's hair, and placed his magnificent top hat on the child's head. The boy spontaneously removed the hat, stuffed the rabbit into it and plopped it back on. He gave the gentleman a toothy smile.

'Tank ya, sir.'

'You are very welcome, my lad,' and at that very moment the all-clear siren sounded. Instantly the mass of humanity began its flight up the many levels of stairs. My elegant gentleman vanished in the crowd."

"Did you ever see the man again?" I asked.

"No, unfortunately, but I saw the child a few weeks later. He was wearing the top hat. It balanced on his little ears. When he removed it, his raggedy old rabbit popped out."

Chapter Eight

I suddenly realized there was complete silence outside. Had it stopped? I held my breath and waited for the all-clear sirens. Finally, after what seemed forever, they blared. Later I would learn we had all survived one of the worst bombings on London so far, and Tillie had succeeded in distracting me during it.

When Dad pushed back the canvas a grey morning light swept into the shelter. Particles of dust rushed through the opening and flew about us. An acrid smell of burning wood and wet cement filled the air. The night noises had been replaced with ambulance and fire engine bells clanging, people shouting and A.R.P. warden whistling.

With Toffee in my arms I rushed out from the dreaded shelter. A layer of fine ash covered the entire back yard. It resembled a fading negative of an old photograph. Our house was standing, but across the road a pile of smoldering timber and bricks was all that remained of our neighbor's once sturdy little brick cottage. Firefighters were dousing the last of the embers. Water flowed down the street from the ruins of our neighbor's home. Large puddles collected in the road, and debris floated about.

Their shelter was damaged, but still stood. They had been saved. Our neighbors stared at the devastation in disbelief. Practically all they owned had been destroyed. Possibly their only clothes were those they wore. Then the reality of the events hit me.

"Mum, it could have been our house," I blurted.

"But it wasn't so don't fret," she answered. Her normally pink complexion had disappeared, and her face was ashen. Tears welled in her blue eyes. She rubbed her right hand across her forehead as though she had a pounding headache.

My father took in the events. His face reddened, his eyes blazed, and his hands gripped in fists. He bit his lower lip so hard I feared he would bleed. I had never seen my father so enraged.

My father roared. "That's it! He's going to the north to Auntie Nan's. We were fools to think the Nazis wouldn't't attack us."

My mother nodded silently and began to cry. He put his arm around her shoulder. She looked up to him and tried to smile.

"Margaret, it will be for the best. Make plans, he's leaving within a *fortnight*."

"Yes, George, it's best for him."

I could not believe it. They were talking about me as though I wasn't standing in front of them. They had made the decision without even asking me. I was angry.

"Mum, Dad, what are you talking about?"

"You are going back north to your aunt's."

"No! I will not leave, not again!" My face became inflamed.

Dad released my mother and faced me.

"You have no say in this, Peter."

"Daddy, please no! Let me stay," I pleaded.

"We should never have listened to the pathetic stories you wrote us when you were away at your Aunt's."

"But Daddy, I wasn't happy there and…"

"Don't you understand? Happiness is a small price to pay for with your life."

Those were his final words. I let out a groan. He walked away with his head high, and his back rigid and straight. I knew this posture. It meant the argument had definitely ended. He crossed the road, and upon reaching our neighbors, grasped their hands. A conversation ensued. Frequently they motioned toward the remains that had once been their home. I wondered what they were talking about, and hoped

I wasn't the subject. An A.R.P. warden came over to them and obviously informed them that they were allowed to enter the bombed area to salvage what little they might find among the debris. This was all too much for me.

My eyes began to sting and tears fell. I felt like a baby. I didn't know what I wanted. I hated being in the shelter, but I hated the thought of leaving my family like a coward. And I hated what awaited me in the north. I hated this war. I stayed looking at the scene in front of me and grew angrier and sadder, and much more confused.

Mum had been watching my father as well. She softly spoke.

"Peter, he wants you to be safe."

She turned and slowly walked into our house.

I continued holding Toffee, and dropped my head down into her soft fur. I did not want Tillie to see my tears. She was so strong. Tillie came to my side. She placed her hands on my shoulders, pulled me to her, and whispered into my ear.

"Shh, Peter, we'll make this right."

Tillie believed she could always fix things for me, and usually did. I shook my head. "No, Tillie, this is one time even you cannot fix things."

She dropped her hands, her arms fell limply at her sides, and for a fleeting moment my brave Tillie looked defeated. She shook her head, and followed in the direction my father had taken.

Still holding Toffee, I ran into our house and took the stairs two at a time. I placed Toffee on the bed and sat next to her. My stomach felt like a barrel of water sloshing about on the deck of a sailing ship in a rough ocean. I thought I might bring up last night's supper. I looked for my waste basket. Instead, I found my other shoe. The sun was streaming through my bedroom window and a sun beam fell on it.

I had forgotten that I was still wearing only one shoe. I removed it, and turned both over. Their soles were wearing out. We hadn't received any shoe rations yet. My school uniform of navy woolen shorts, white shirt, and blue striped tie was slung over a chair. I had almost outgrown the jacket, but it didn't matter. I shook my head. Even if the family received ration tickets for one, I didn't want it.

Everything was being rationed. Ration books had been distributed to every household. Unless we had tickets for an item, there was no getting it. What a way to live. Everything from underwear to *petrol* was being rationed. Before this horrid war we could get anything we wanted and needed. Yesterday Mum had to queue up to buy sugar. Tillie couldn't purchase her silk stockings because the war effort needed silk to make parachutes. Dad had stopped driving the car, and rode a bicycle everywhere. It had been ages since I had even seen a banana, and when was the last time I had eaten an orange?

"Soon there won't be butter or marmalade for my toast. I even have to measure how many dog *biscuits* I give you, Toffee."

Would things ever be the same? What would happen if Hitler won the war? I didn't want to think about it. But what if Great Britain did lose, would things be the same? My life would be changed forever. I would have to join the Nazi's horrid youth group, and walk about in a ridiculous *goose step*. Would I survive this war? A tremendous weight pressed down upon me. The idea of going to school was the very last thing I wanted.

Maybe I should go north and live with my aunt. I lowered my body onto the bed. I threw an arm over my eyes and remained still. Toffee nuzzled me. I stroked her, and she sighed. For the first time since the sirens had sounded last night the dog relaxed.

"Poor Toffee, the bombing is driving you *batty* too. I know how you feel old girl. If they do force me to go to Carlisle I promise I'll take you along."

I was resting this way when Mum came into the room.

"Peter, you haven't dressed for school."

"Mum, I don't feel like going to school today. Can I stay home?" I begged.

She sat on my bed and looked out the window at the scene across the road. After a while she turned her head, reached over, and gently pushed the hair off my forehead. I felt great tenderness from her caress, and it gave me some temporary relief.

"Come along, Peter, get dressed. We'll have a cup of tea and talk about this. Come on, you too, Toffee."

She left us. I slowly rose from the bed, washed up, dressed, and went downstairs into the sunlit kitchen. Toffee found a dab of sunlight on the floor and began circling it until she located the perfect spot and settled down. I sat at the table while Mum put the kettle on. I carefully spooned an exact amount of tea leaves into the teapot. While she waited for the water to boil, Mum toasted a few pieces of day-old bread, and then poured the hot water over the tea leaves. I watched her carefully spread marmalade over the toast, and noticed that the three pieces she placed in front of me were thickly covered with the orange preserves, while her one piece had hardly any jam on it. Mum was always going with less so that we could have more. Suddenly I felt outraged and pounded my fist on the table. Tea spilt out of the pot, and Mum placed her hand over mine.

"Enough of this, Peter, it will serve no purpose to be so angry."

"Well I am angry. I am angry that we can't buy things unless we have enough ration tickets. I am angry that I have to practically count each tea leaf when making tea. I am angry that you are denying yourself food so that I have more. I don't get proper sleep anymore, and even Toffee is not happy. I am angry that our lives are being turned upside down."

"Yes, our lives have been turned upside down. Things are out of our control. We must accept it and move along. We have no choice, Peter."

"Mum, nothing is the same anymore!"

She was holding her cup of tea up to her lips and looked over its rim at me. She set the cup down and quietly answered.

"No, since the Nazis have launched their *Blitzkrieg* on London nothing is the same anymore. But that doesn't mean you have to ruin your life and go *barmy* over it."

"What if England loses the war, what if Hitler wins, what if…"

"What if all those things that you are worrying about don't happen, Peter? Look back into history, Great Britain has always won."

"Sorry, Mum, but you've got that wrong. What happened in America?"

We both laughed, and for a brief moment the tension was lifted.

"Peter, did you hate living with Auntie Nan so very much?"

Mum surprised me when she asked this question. It was completely out of the blue, and it took me a while to answer.

"No, Auntie Nan's really super. Things just weren't---"

I couldn't explain, and I allowed my last sentence to melt away. Mum didn't pursue it, instead she took a different tact.

"Your father and I want you out of harm's way. This bombing is not going to let up. In all probability, it will get much worse. We made a mistake when we let you come home. Your father is very upset that you talked us into letting you return. Please understand. Your wellbeing is our first concern."

"But we have the Anderson shelter and---"

When I said this Mum clicked her tongue. This was her usual response when she disagreed with a statement. I waited for her response, and it came with tremendous force.

"And what, Peter? I'm sorry, but I feel we are not being fair to you. Don't you think that when the Anderson shelter crashed down on you, things were altered greatly? Each night we spend in the shelter is torture for you. As parents, we realize your suffering. Perhaps, Peter, London is not a safe haven for you."

I had no answer. I thought I was doing a fairly good job hiding my fears, but apparently not. My parents saw through me, and I felt terrible realizing that even Tillie knew that I was a coward. I was afraid to go north, and I was afraid to enter the shelter. There were no answers. I felt my face flush, and I knew my ears were turning red as well. Mum watched me and then stood up. She called to Toffee and went to the back door.

"Toffee and I are going for a walk. Your lunch is on the table, but if you decide not to go to school, it's alright. I'll send a note to school tomorrow."

She walked out with Toffee in pursuit. Through the kitchen window I watched them go up the road in the opposite direction of the school. Mum was giving me time to think.

I went back upstairs and looked out my window again. Across the road, Tillie was helping Dad and the neighbors. They had recovered a chair and a stool, and a few other items which they had lined up on the walk. Tillie was wiping the chair clean with an old rag, and all the while she was whistling a nameless tune. Even this simple task became a heroic act in Tillie's hands. I envied her ability to face life with such an attitude. I looked for my father, and saw him pulling at a wooden chest from under a charred beam. His face was still grim, and I knew that he was undoubtedly thinking that this could have been our house and our belongings, but it wasn't.

"Yes, things could definitely be worse," I said to no one.

I tossed my books into my bag and tied the gas mask to it. Since mustard gas had been used during WWI it was thought the Nazis would use it again. I remembered Doe's letter and hoped her dad was right. Carrying the masks was a nuisance, especially since we weren't even sure they'd work against whatever gas the Nazis had developed to use on us. We were always having drills at school, and I hated putting the blasted thing on.

The rubber smell probably was worse than any gas Hitler could drop on us, and I felt confined with it covering my face. I wondered if I would ever have to seriously use it.

Once again, I ran downstairs and into the kitchen. I tucked my sandwich and an apple in my bag and was on my way. There was still plenty of time to get to school before the first bell rang. Besides, since the bombing had begun things were even different in school. Punctuality was not so essential any more. Being there was, because you'd made it through the night.

I headed out the door, through the garden and open gate. Down the road Mum was talking to one of the A.R.P wardens, while Toffee was busy rummaging around an indistinguishable piece of gutted furniture. Mum saw me and waved.

"See you at tea time," I shouted to her. She smiled and nodded.

I covered the distance quickly while thinking it was a good thing I have long legs.

It was a warm autumn day. The sun was shining and it would have been a perfect day for a picnic, but the scene about me wasn't pleasant. There was evidence of the night's bombing everywhere.

Chapter Nine

began looking for my best *mate*, David, who lived a few roads down. Before the bombings began, we always met at the same place and time each day and walked to school together. But the recent nightly bombings had changed even that routine.

Today I worried he might not be at the appointed spot. David's parents were still waiting for their shelter to be delivered, and his family took cover in the cupboard under the stairs. Would they survive a blast if their house was hit? How much protection is a flight of steps? The image of the neighbor's demolished cottage flashed vividly across my eyes. I felt my heart race as this picture projected in my head. I dispelled these ideas from my thoughts and instead allowed my memory to reflect on our first day in nursery school several years ago.

I recall being extremely excited about going to school, and feeling quite grown up wearing my newly acquired school uniform. I was dressed in a tan blazer, with matching short pants and a beige shirt and brown tie. On my head, I wore a brown cap with the school's insignia. All the way to school my mother chatted on about how now I was "a big boy" and would have to behave like one. At that exact moment, I had no idea what she meant. To ask her would have led to a lengthy explanation. Nevertheless, I decided to question her, but before I could my mother pointed ahead of us.

"There's the school, Peter," she said.

Down the road children were running into the schoolyard directly in front of the one-story grey building. The school was constructed of multi-tone grey stone and brick, with two huge front doors. On each door, a weathered coat of arms was barely visible. They were built of a dark wood, with three wide bands of brass running horizontally across each one. Interior green shades were pulled a quarter of the way down each tall window that lined the facade of the building. In the back of the school two tall brick chimneys puffed out pale clouds of smoke. Several soaring chestnut trees grew majestically around the school, and everything appeared so very massive, while I felt so very small.

Even the youngsters in the yard looked much bigger than I. They seemed rather happy to be going to school, because they were laughing and shouting to each other. This encouraged me. We went to the side of the building where a group of mothers with children my age was waiting. In comparison to the older children, they were teary eyed with runny noses and sad faces. We took our place in line behind a mother and her little girl who was sitting on the ground and carrying on something terrible. She stomped her feet on the cement. She grabbed at her mother's skirt. She cried pathetically. None of this distracted her mum who just maintained a steady conversation with the lady in front of them.

I tightly held onto my own mother's hand, pulled at it, and looked up to see how she was reacting to this sorrowful display. She smiled down at me, tickled me under my chin, and whispered in my ear.

"She's not behaving grown up."

Okay, I thought, crying and acting horrid means behaving like a baby.

"Don't worry, Mum. You won't find me doing that," I promised.

I brought myself to the present, and realized this very morning I had cried when my father announced his decision to send me back to my aunt's. I was a thirteen-year-old behaving like a baby. I shook my head and allowed myself to continue with my daydreams. I remembered how we waited in line until a tall, stout woman wearing a pair of spectacles on a string around her neck approached our group.

"Good morning, children. My name is Mrs. Dunn and I shall be your teacher. Mothers, you may leave now, since I will take the little ones into school."

My mother kissed me on the forehead, and patted my shoulder.

"Ta Ta, love. Remember what we spoke about."

Then with all the other mothers she quickly walked away. She looked back once and waved, but that was it. I had been left with a group of strange children. I was abandoned. Before I could call out to her, we were guided by the teacher and marched into the school. My eyes started to water and my lower lip quiver, but I would not cry. I would not behave like a baby.

The teacher led us to a large room. The walls were painted light blue, with colorful pictures of animals and flowers on the walls. A large open toy box was under a window, and a net bag of blocks rested on the floor next to it. The teacher's desk was in front of the room, and directly behind it was a black board with white chalk letters neatly printed on it. A circle of small chairs had been arranged in the middle of the room, and in front of each chair was a little yellow cardboard box.

In an unusually loud voice, Mrs. Dunn addressed us,

"Now children, kindly line up along the wall. When I call your name, please raise your hand, say 'present', and then go sit in the chair to which I point. In front of the chair you are occupying is a box for each of you."

The sniffling and crying continued throughout this entire process, but this did not stop Mrs. Dunn. She continued calling names and pointing to chairs until eventually she called my name.

"Peter Morris?"

"Present" I squeaked, as I hurried to the chair Mrs. Dunn pointed to for me.

Most children had opened their yellow boxes and peered into them, while others were so miserable they left them unopened at their feet. I picked up my box, which contained several colored crayons, blank paper, and an apple. We were all miserable, but I was determined to be grown up.

My place was between a small blond-haired girl who was sitting perfectly straight and a thin boy with red hair. The girl stared intensely at the teacher. She didn't appear to mind that she was now alone among strangers. The boy had stopped crying, but his tear stained face now matched his copper hair. He wiped his eyes, blew his nose in a small crumbled handkerchief, and slouched further down in his chair.

I wanted my mother so desperately, but knew that by now she was home and there was no way to reach her.

"Mustn't be a baby," I said aloud.

At this, the boy swiveled in his seat. He looked at me hard and long. Then without any warning, he hit me, so I instinctively hit back. We immediately began to whimper, and then we were both crying loudly. Mrs. Dunn had been looking down at the list of children still to be called, but upon hearing our cries, her head jerked up. She hastened over to us.

"What is going on with you two boys?" She asked in a very stern voice.

"He hit me!" We answered simultaneously.

"Young man, David, is it? Did you hit your classmate?" Mrs. Dunn asked my attacker.

"Yes!" the red-haired boy answered in a sniveling voice.

"Why, David?" Mrs. Dunn continued.

"He called me a baby!" He sobbed.

"David, that is no reason to hit someone. That was very naughty." Mrs. Dunn then addressed me.

"Peter, did you hit David?"

"Yes, because he hit me first."

I had difficulty answering because I was gulping for air between my bawling.

"Is it true that you called him a baby?" she questioned.

"No. I didn't. I wasn't even talking to him. I was talking to myself, and remembering what my mum told me, not to behave like a baby."

The classroom had become very quiet. All the crying and whimpering had stopped, while about twenty pairs of eyes focused on us. The children forgot their despair, and were fascinated by the drama unfolding in front of them. Mrs. Dunn reached down, took each of our right hands in hers and brought both our little hands together. Then in a very kind voice addressed us.

"Boys, there will be no fighting in my classroom. David, you heard incorrectly. Peter was reminding himself not to be a baby, not you. This was all a misunderstanding. Now shake hands, say you are sorry, and forget this ever happened."

And that is how David and I became best friends. Since that day several years ago we have spent most of our waking hours together. We played together and studied together. We caused mischief and got into trouble together. We laughed and even cried together. We were inseparable. Then war was declared, and I was sent to my aunt's farm, and David to a small village outside of Lancaster.

David never was any good at writing letters, and I missed him terribly. At least I was living with my aunt, but David, like so many evacuees, was *billeted* with strangers. He was sent to live with an elderly couple whose son was in the *R.A.F.* They were nice enough and treated him rather well, but he'd never been away from home, so it was very difficult living with people he'd never met before. Neither of us liked being separated from our parents.

My thoughts came to a crashing halt when I reached our meeting place and David was nowhere in sight. His house was not visible from our rendezvous spot, but in the sky over the road where he lived a thick haze of black smoke billowed. I became uneasy as the minutes passed and he did not show. Was he okay? I smelled the all too familiar stench caused by fire's destruction. Where was he? What was I doing just standing around waiting for my friend? I started running in the direction of his house. The smell intensified, and the smoke continued to rise as it drifted slowly north. I threw my book bag to the ground to pick up speed without the heavy load of my bag.

I turned the corner to David's house and stopped. In the middle of his road firemen were dousing the remains of an old *lorry* which a few minutes earlier had probably been engulfed in flames. David came into view from around the wreckage. He saw me, smiled, saluted, and slowly made his way to me. His cheerful face showed the stress of another sleepless night. Under his hazel eyes were dark half circles. His red hair flew in different directions, his unknotted tie hung loosely from his neck, his shirt was askew having been buttoned up wrong, his pants looked like he had slept in them, and he had on mismatched socks.

"David! You look awful!" I said as I hurried to him.

Always a joker, David tried to flatten his hair, and in an upper crust accent answered.

"Just got off the polo field. Didn't have time to freshen up, dear chap."

"What happened here?"

"About an hour ago the *lorry* came to pack up our neighbor's furniture, cause they're moving to Buckinghamshire. Lucky thing for them, the crew hadn't loaded anything into it when the fire started."

"Did it get bombed?"

"Bombed! Peter, *blimey*, can't you think of anything else? Normal things like a careless fire still do happen in London. One of the *blokes* dropped his cigarette on a pile of oily tarps in the back, and the whole thing went up in smoke."

He started laughing, and as usual it was contagious. I began laughing with him over the situation and also over my unnecessary worries for him.

We watched the firemen pack up their equipment and pile it onto the fire engine. They looked completely exhausted. The fatigue in their bodies was evident to the crowd that had watched them working. Their faces were covered with the grime and soot of the many fires they had encountered during the night and early morning. The uniforms of several were scorched, and ripped. Poor chaps had probably been up the entire night putting out fires in the area. They were slumped against the fire engine when an elderly white-haired lady carrying a huge tray approached them.

The tray was set very formally with a white cloth and serviettes, a bone-china pot of tea, matching cups and saucers, and a plate heaped high with sandwiches. We heard her speak to them in a voice that was years younger than her age.

"Hello there. I imagine you boys haven't had a proper bite for hours. How would you like a cup of tea and a little something to eat?"

The tired firemen each nodded silently to her. We were so enthralled with the little lady that we had not noticed the old gentleman who followed her. He was carrying a small table which he set down in the middle of the street. The woman placed the tray on the table and motioned to the firemen to help themselves. They thanked the elderly couple and tucked into the sandwiches and tea. She had speculated correctly; the men were starving for within a few minutes the plate was empty and the tea pot drained dry.

"Would you like some more?" the woman asked.

"No, thank you, Missus, this was very kind." One of the firemen answered for all of them.

"Nonsense, you boys deserve this and more. Without you London would go up in smoke," her husband responded.

There were murmurs of agreement from those who had been watching. The firemen smiled modestly to them, as they climbed onto the fire engine. I remembered my two traveling companions, the twins, Tommy and Alice, and how proud they were of their fireman father who was probably fighting fires throughout the city. The elderly gentleman was indeed correct, for without these men what would become of London?

One of the firemen pulled the rope of the bell and clanged it loudly. Somehow, he played the first chords of *Rule Britannia,* the crowd cheered and waved, and the fire truck drove off. The burnt *lorry* remained in the middle of the road.

We walked around the charred frame. The entire back had burned, and all that was left was the burnt front cab. Looking down, I found a *sixpence* among the ashes, picked it up and pocketed it.

"Nice find, we'll stop at the sweet shop on our way home and buy some licorice strings."

David grinned in approval, and with the tip of his shoe poked around the debris at our feet. He whistled a low note when he discovered his mismatched socks.

"How did that happen?"

"Guess you have another pair like them at home," I laughed.

"Yeah!" David giggled.

We reached the spot where I had dropped my book bag, I picked it up and flung it over my shoulder.

"David, you haven't told me yet how you did last night," I said.

"*Blimey*! I thought they'd never stop," he answered.

"Our neighbor's cottage took a direct hit. There's not much left of it."

"Wooo, poor folks. You must have felt that one in the shelter."

"Yes, it even woke up Tillie. How about you?"

"We were lucky last night, but I didn't get much sleep. I despise those home defense *ack-acks* and the blasted noise they make all night long. You know, I don't think they brought down one *Messerschmitt* or Heinkel."

"Do you think the lads who aim the *ack-acks* got any target practice with those guns before they began shooting at the real thing?"

He chuckled and immediately we were both hooting over my silly question. After we quieted down, my next words unfortunately changed our mood.

"David, my parents are sending me away again. I'm to leave within a *fortnight*."

He studied my face, shrugged his shoulders and spoke in an unusually very serious voice.

"Yes, mine are talking that way too."

"Where will you go this time, David?"

"I don't know. Maybe to my sister and her husband in Ireland."

"Ireland! That would mean you would be miles away."

"Right, and some of them will be miles of water."

I'd not anticipated this. How could his parents do this to him, to us?

"David, if they send you to Ireland you may be there for ages."

"Yes."

David remained silent for a while until as if talking to himself, he softly muttered,

"Maybe we should have stayed away from London and not returned. You know, we would have been safe away from this *Blitz*."

"What! We were cowards leaving our families behind. No, never. I did that once and don't want to do it again."

"You might have no choice," David mumbled.

I hated how David had a way of always saying something that upset me, and at the same time got me thinking. This was one of those times.

Chapter Ten

Our conversation had come to a screeching halt when suddenly David asked the same question my mother had.

"Peter, why did you really hate living with your Auntie Nan? I know what you told me, about being bored, but I never bought that. Living on a farm and dealing with animals is the least boring thing in the world, especially for a chap whose whole life has been in London."

My thoughts whirled back to the months I had spent in Carlisle, but I didn't respond. We walked together in silence for a while, and then I told him about Colin when a fire engine with its bell clanging came tearing down the road. The truck made a sudden stop, and we were practically thrown off our feet by the firemen who jumped from their fire engine and onto the path immediately in front of us. An *Air Raid Precaution* Warden met them and a heated conversation ensued. They gave directions to the warden to clear the area of onlookers and cautiously approached the house.

The A.R.P. warden was shouting at the top of his lungs and blowing his shrill whistle. "Please everyone, stand clear. There's an undetonated *incendiary bomb* in the front yard. Come along now, don't loiter, kindly move on!"

During the night thousands of *incendiary bombs* had been dropped proving extremely destructive and unbelievably effective. Massive fires had erupted all over London, causing the light resulting from these fires to serve as beacons for the enemy bombers and their escorts. As the Nazis flew through the dark skies, the enemy bombers were able to locate their targets, and drop their explosives onto the city. Frequently, however, an *incendiary bomb* would drop, but not explode. This was the case today.

Like the other bystanders, we had no intention of complying with the warden's request to 'kindly move on'. We cautiously remained a safe distance from the house and watched the firemen in action. This was a nasty job for them. These bombs were unpredictable and could go off at any time. The firemen could be very badly burned, and unfortunately this happened all too frequently.

They had pulled out their hoses and were drowning the bomb in huge amounts of water, only stopping when they were satisfied enough water had been poured on it. One of the firemen explained to the A.R.P. warden that the bomb would have to be kept wet until someone from the Army Service Corps came to defuse it. The owner of the house overheard this, and immediately began a quarrel with the warden who previously had told the family they could not return to the house.

"An' just who do ye think is to keep the blasted thing wet?" the irate owner asked.

David looked at me and whispered.

"Poor choice of adjective when referring to the 'blasted' thing."

This remark made me momentarily forget his earlier accusations.

In the distance, we heard a church bell ring and counted the bongs. Eight! We had to hurry along and not let anything else stop us. But we were not prepared for what we would encounter along the way.

Down the road we came upon a sight of utter destruction. Several houses had been hit, resulting in huge gaping holes where homes had once stood. The contents of the houses were in shambles, yet inexplicitly amongst all the debris a single article would often be standing completely unharmed. We stared into the ruins, amazed how the morning sun's rays hit a gilded mirror standing on its side completely intact. It was macabre how it perfectly reflected the devastation surrounding it.

The inhabitants of the houses stared numbly at the remains of their homes. Several women sat on the curb of the road. A young woman wearing only a bathrobe and slippers rocked back and forth in anguish. In her hands, she held pieces of what once had been a toy wooden soldier.

A young man wearing torn pajamas limped toward her. When she raised her face to him it was covered with the filth from the explosion.

Tracks of tears ran down her cheeks. She had been crying in silence. The man sat on the curb next to her and pulled her to him. Immediately her entire body shook with passionate sobs of unbelievable sorrow. Behind her their Anderson shelter had been blown out from its foundation and lay in a twisted heap in their yard.

David nudged me and asked, "Do you think anyone survived that?"

I choked on my answer, "I don't know."

He was incredulous.

"But I thought they were supposed to protect people from bombs."

I could not believe his ignorance.

"Not if it takes a direct hit."

"I didn't know."

We slowly moved away. Stunned, we passed a group of men who regarded the carnage in disbelief. Their clothes were wrinkled and dirty, and their faces had the exhausted look of a wakeful night. One muttered under his breath and punched his right hand into the palm of his left. I wanted to tell him that I felt his anger. I knew how his whole body ached from the sights he witnessed, but I kept on walking.

Two ambulances had parked in the midst of the confusion, and Red Cross personnel tendered to the injured. A path from one of the houses had a darkish stain splattered across it. I immediately looked away. All around us my greatest fears had become reality. An older boy and girl gazed at me in despair, but I had no words for them. They didn't try to hide the tears streaming down their faces. The sport of war was no longer a game played in the school yard. It was very real now. Only the very small children didn't seem to mind the changes in their surroundings.

A laughing toddler pulled on a rope that cordoned off a bombed area. He was amused how when he tugged the rope sharply the wrecked fence moved up and down. His laughter rang through the misery in an eerie way. I hastened to leave. A tiny girl smiled at us as we passed. She had found her doll's *pram* and was trying to push it unsuccessfully since it had lost a wheel. Her face was alight with happiness.

What did she have to be happy about? Her life would never be the same. The coroner's van had pulled up in front of the pile of bricks and timber from which she had uncovered the *pram*. A white-haired woman who was watching over her ushered her away from the scene.

We heard the child question, "Granny, where's mum?"

I did not wait for the answer. I could not escape the reality of the previous night's *Blitz*. Hitler and his *Luftwaffe* had bombed London without concern for civilian life. The plan was very clear. Destroy London and all its inhabitants.

A row of shops had been hit, including the sweet shop where we had intended to spend my found money. I looked at the colored glass that covered the street. Just yesterday sour balls, licorice strings, caramels and other penny *sweets* stored in tall tinted glass jars lined the shelves of the shop. Today hundreds of colored glass pieces mixed with a sticky mess covered the cracked pavement.

"Guess we'll save the money for another day," I told David.

"I'm really not in the mood for licorice anymore," David answered.

Every shop on the road had massive damage. All that remained of the bakery was its huge oven. A few bricks had fallen off it, but it still looked workable. Several people were observing the damage, and I overheard one say,

"If the baker can get flour, we might still be able to have bread for our tea."

The others didn't reply to this statement. I imagined they were thinking of the enormity of the war versus a loaf of warm bread.

The bookstore's contents had survived the bombing, but not the rush of water the fire brigade had used to extinguish the resulting blaze of the building. Water logged books and papers were strewn everywhere. I looked down at my feet where a drenched copy of *A Tale of Two Cities* lay open.

"No, this is a tale of one city, our London," I thought aloud. An icy breeze swept over me, and I buttoned my jacket tightly against the sudden autumn chill.

David looked equally as miserable as he stepped over the scattered papers and books.

"Pity, this was my favorite book store," he muttered softly.

I scanned the interior of the shop and gave a low sigh. Suddenly I heard a bird chirping above the dull noise of our surroundings. Further down the road a house had its front rooms blown away. I could see into the first floor with the kitchen and dining room in the rear. In the kitchen, a caged yellow canary was hopping from one perch to another, and its clear voice gave credence to another day.

Upstairs a back bedroom was exposed. Resembling flags flying in the wind, clothes streamed out of a wardrobe. The bathroom door hung dangerously on a single hinge and suspended over the ruined garden below. Someone obviously had been preparing a bath and forgot to turn the water off when the raid began. Water spilled from the tub creating a waterfall of sorts tumbling down the still standing side of the house.

A boy about our age stood in what had once been the parlor room. He pulled a charred *cricket* bat out from the debris, studied it and threw it back onto the littered floor. He cautiously entered the kitchen, and unhooked the bird cage from its stand. Carrying the cage, he walked toward his parents who stood with blank faces watching and waiting. For what?

David shook his head. "Poor *bloke*, his *cricket* days are over."

I answered, "Yeah, but at least he still has his bird."

The adjoining house had sustained minor damage. The side windows had been blown out, and the owners were already busy boarding them up. A maple tree next to the house had been split in two exposing a squirrel's nest balancing precariously on a broken bough.

"I wonder if the squirrel made it?" David asked light heartedly.

To our amazement a scruffy grey squirrel sprang out from under the branches of the half-fallen tree. The animal jumped onto the still standing trunk, scampered up and practically flew into the nest. Then for several minutes only its bedraggled tail was visible. Eventually it leaped out from the nest, ran down the tree, onto the ground, and disappeared through the back garden.

"Guess it decided to find new *digs*," David said.

"Clever squirrel," I answered.

"Yeah, smarter than us," David concluded.

He turned in the direction of the school, but I was rooted to the spot. I stared down the path the little animal had taken. David called to me in an attempt at joviality.

"Hey *mate*, what are you thinking of doing? Joining the squirrel? Come on, we're going to be late."

"If I could find a nice big oak tree, in the middle of a quiet forest, I just might do that," I told David.

He gave me a slow grin. I kicked a scorched can in front of us, and he immediately joined in the diversion. But this didn't last long. When we turned the corner toward our school's road we were stopped by a *bobby* who ordered us to cross over to the other side of the street. A huge crater was gaping in the middle of the road, and an ambulance had driven right into it. Its *bonnet* was completely hidden inside the hole, and its rear wheels were sticking out. Luckily it was empty.

A crowd had gathered and watched two mechanics who were trying desperately to haul the ambulance out. They managed to pull it up a bit when suddenly there was a shout.

"Hey there, somethin' comin' out of the exhaust. *Blimey*! Ye forgot to turn the blooming thing off."

Fumes were definitely billowing out the exhaust. The motor was still running! They couldn't possibly haul it out. Anything could happen, including a fire.

Without any hesitation, the smaller of the two mechanics lowered himself into the hole. He twisted his body as he tried unsuccessfully to get through the broken window. I heard him griping as he turned his shoulders around to make another attempt at entering. After several futile maneuvers, he slowly backed out and heaved himself onto the road. Bits of glass had fallen into his thinning hair giving him the appearance of wearing a shiny halo. He shook his head, dusted himself off, and walked to his partner. After consulting for a few minutes, they ambled up to us.

"How would one of ye like ta earn a *shilling*?"

"What do we gotta do?" David asked.

"The *bonnet* of the ambulance smashed into the dash, so the window's blocked and I can't get through. But you're thin enough."

He was looking directly at me! The thought of going down into that hole was terrifying. The metal hulk of the ambulance was no different than our shelter. How could I possibly go down head first into the dark? I wouldn't be able to breath in such a small space? There was no way I could possibly do this!

"Um, I'm not sure I can get down there. I don't know if I can ahh…"

People in the crowd had overheard the conversation and were conferring with their neighbors that this was a logical solution. All eyes were on me, and suddenly I felt ill. I gasped for air, pulled at my collar, and loosened my tie which suddenly felt like it was strangling me. I felt uncomfortably warm, and my forehead was covered with perspiration, so I used the back of my sleeve to wipe it dry. David had been studying me curiously when he cheerfully announced,

"Listen, *mate*, no problem, I'll do it. I'm smaller than you."

He gave my arm a thud, winked, and with the mechanics walked toward the crash. They began explaining where the ignition was and how to cut off the motor. He nodded several times as he listened intently to their instructions. Confident he understood their directions, they patted him on the back and lowered him into the hole. I sheepishly approached to see how David was doing. His head disappeared as he squirmed his way into the vehicle, and within seconds he managed to get his shoulders through the tight entry while his feet stuck out of the broken window. Both men went down on their knees and asked him to describe what he saw. David mumbled something that made the two men laugh loudly, but then he shouted some unintelligible question which apparently made sense to the mechanics. Together they stuck their heads deeper into the hole and simultaneously gave directions.

David complained, "I can't see! You two *blokes* are blocking the light and it is dark enough in here."

They immediately withdrew, and almost instantly the motor stopped. David had done it!

"Would the two of you mind getting me out? It's bloody hot down here," he shouted.

The larger of the two mechanics grabbed David's feet and carefully pulled him out, but not before David somehow managed to triumphantly clang the ambulance bell. The watching crowd let out a collective cheer once he had emerged from the ambulance. Feeling quite pleased with himself, and thoroughly enjoying the attention, beaming David took a deep bow, and slipped the promised *shilling* into his pocket. With the bearing of a victorious warrior, he sauntered over to me.

I had to congratulate his achievement, even though I was secretly jealous of his performance.

"Nicely done, David."

"All in a day's work, *mate*," he boasted.

He had every reason to be smug.

Billy and Albert, two of our classmates, who had joined the crowd and seen the entire operation called to David who motioned them to join us as we trudged along to school. This resulted in much congratulatory pounding on David's back and flattering remarks. But the sights around me suddenly took second place to David's triumph.

For I alone saw the misery the *Blitzkrieg* had caused. The emptiness I felt was overwhelming. During the night, homes had been reduced to ruins, yet today people were going about as though the horrors of last night had never happened. Shops were opening and women were queuing up in front of them for whatever commodity was available. Retirees were cleaning up their gardens, raking up shrapnel and fragments as though sweeping up autumn leaves, and all the while they chatted gaily to their neighbors. Mothers were pushing sleeping babies in their *prams*. Fathers carrying lunch pails or brief cases were hurrying off to work. Children were running to school before the second bell rang. The world had turned upside down and I was the only one who realized it.

David's entourage had grown, since several other lads hearing what happened joined us. Upon arriving at the schoolyard, the story was repeated many times, and each time the impending danger and David's courage was magnified. He was glowing in the adulation and I had no place at his side.

Chapter Eleven

I walked alone into the school yard and through the massive doors that opened into a wide corridor with classrooms on either side. Slowly, without purpose I entered my classroom, dropped my book bag onto my desk, and lowered myself onto my chair, when I heard my name.

"Hello Peter, how did it go for you last night?" It was Doreen.

Recently whenever Doe spoke to me, my mouth immediately became dry and my palms began to sweat. It's really silly because she's been my friend since my first day of nursery school. Doe stills sits perfectly straight and focused, as though the King himself were speaking. I wish I was as attentive in class. She's the only girl David and I palled around with. She's tremendous fun. When she teased David and me about the oddest things it never hurt. There have been times when Doe became very serious, like when I complained about things being rationed. She explained the importance of it, but I still didn't like the idea, and that really bothered her.

Lately I've been noticing things about her I had never seen before. I never realized she has green flecks in her light brown eyes, or that her skin is the color of fresh cream. When she wants to get her point across, she throws back her head and her hair swishes. Through the years her hair has become darker, and now it is the hue of summer wheat. I've overheard some lads say that to look into her face is like looking at a cinema poster of a Hollywood star. I don't think Doe knows that, but I certainly do.

"Uh, we had quite a bit of activity."

I managed to get these words out of my mouth which now felt like it was full of marbles.

"Oh! So did we, our house lost several windows from a blast."

Doreen said this as calmly as though she was telling me that it had started raining. She amazed me, I was still shaking from the sights I had seen while walking to school. I felt like such a dunce, her windows had been blown out, yet she was as cool as ice. Perhaps I the only one afraid of this war, and the *Blitzkrieg* that threatened us every night.

Suddenly I was consumed with the fear that she might have heard how I had refused to help with the ambulance. What would she think of me? I had to find out whether she had spoken to anyone who was there.

"So, Doe, did you hear anything interesting this morning?"

"No, only that the sweet shop had been blown to pieces. I did like that shop."

"Oh, yeah. I saw it. There's nothing left. Most of the stores on that row were destroyed."

"How dreadful!"

I was about to respond when David and several of the lads who had seen the goings on with the ambulance walked into the room. They were talking and laughing loudly until they saw me and stopped. David was oblivious to this and kept on chatting to no one in particular.

"Sure a nice way to make some money. Just call me if you need to get into a tight spot."

Two lads put their arms around him and tried to lift him, while the others began to sing.

For he's a jolly good fellow! For he's a jolly good fellow! That nobody can deny!

Doreen was puzzled by this outburst of singing.

"What's this all about, Peter?" she asked.

Before I could fabricate an answer, Mr. Blake, our teacher, entered the room.

"Must dash!" Doreen said as she hurried to her desk.

Mr. Blake removed his trench coat and cap, and hung them on a hook near the door. He wiped his bald head with his right hand, and arranged his wire frame glasses on his prominent nose. His brown eyes peered through the spectacles as he surveyed the room. He stretched himself to his full height, and raised his nasal voice above the noise.

"Alright boys, settle down. Gentlemen, would you like to share with the rest of us why David deserves such praise?"

As five voices shouted out their individual descriptions of what David had accomplished, David quietly took his place in the row next to mine. Mr. Blake raised his veined hands in the air to silence the blabbering, and addressed David.

"Perhaps, David, it would be best if you explained the reason for this jubilance."

This was it! David was going to tell everyone that I was a twit who would not go down into the hole and through the ambulance window. I was about to be exposed, and my classmates would know what a coward I was. Our eyes fixed, David shrugged and looked away.

"It wasn't anything. I helped a couple of *blokes* out with their ambulance."

He busied himself emptying his book bag. He had kept my secret, at the expense of his own glory. His admirers tried to praise him further, but Mr. Blake stopped them.

"That's enough. Well done, David. I am quite sure that whatever you did must have been quite congratulatory to receive such laudations from your fellow classmates. Now everyone, stand. Let us bow our heads in silent prayer for all the good men and women who are protecting our country.

We stood at attention in front of the Union Jack, and I silently prayed for all the pilots who flew their *Spitfires* over us at night. I asked that they return to the ground unharmed. Mr. Blake raised a pitch to his mouth, blew into it and began us in song.

God save our gracious King,
Long live our noble King,

I sang, and several times I cracked when trying to reach the high notes, but I made up for it by singing as loudly as I could.

Scatter his enemies
And make them fall…;

It gave me a sense of pride that in schools across Great Britain children were singing to "scatter his enemies and make them fall". I thought about the talk Mum and I had this morning and felt a little more optimistic. We would win this war!

Once we sat down we realized there were two empty seats which usually were occupied by Bess and Grace, two cousins. They lived with their families in a large house a few roads over from David. Mr. Blake stood behind his desk, and drummed his long fingers on its top. He cleared his voice and began speaking in a very serious tone.

"Children, two of your classmates are not with us," he began.

Upon saying these words, he realized we were all thinking the worst, because our faces had turned ashen, and there was deadening silence in the room.

"Let me assure you that they are quite well, but their parents have decided to send them away to relatives in Scotland. We wish them a safe journey."

A murmur of relief ran through the class, and he had to raise his hand to silence us. Once we had quieted down, Mr. Blake began writing on the black board. With his back to us he gave us directions.

"Kindly, take out your math homework, and let us see how you all did."

This was fascinating. Last night we had been bombed to bits. Two of our classmates had been basically banished to the north, but our homework still had to be reviewed and corrected. What a mad world we were living in.

I could not pay attention to the instruction. I was considering what had just been told to us by Mr. Blake. Other parents were once again taking steps to send their children out of London for safety, just like David's and mine were planning.

Another thought soon took form, David had shielded me today, he was truly my best *mate*. How could I ever repay him for his silence? Several times during the morning he caught my eye and nodded. I smiled in return. The lesson dragged on, and I tried desperately to concentrate, but wasn't successful.

Finally, Mr. Blake completed the math session and proceeded to geography. This interested me, and I was able to focus. Since the war had begun geography lessons had taken on another aspect. We learned about the terrain of the different countries, and the difficulties military men encountered when climbing mountains, crossing rivers or trying to find cover in vast fields of farm land. A huge map of the world had been nailed to the wall. Tiny black flags had been pinned wherever the enemy was or had invaded, and small red flags showed where British troops had been deployed

There were many more black flags across the map of Europe than there were red flags. Besides Germany, Austria, Poland and Italy, black flags now were positioned in Czechoslovakia, France, Luxembourg, Denmark, Norway and the list was growing. It was scary to look at this map, but every morning we referred to it and based on the information over the *wireless* we added flags. None had been removed yet. Mr. Blake told us that eventually the two colors would be mixed together which meant Britain and her allies would be fighting the invaders back across the borders. The most important thing for all of us was that there were no black flags in England.

I wanted to get to David and thank him for keeping my secret before any of the other fellows got to him during lunch. I needed to talk to him about Bess and Grace, and how they had been evacuated. I had to share with him my idea that if other parents were sending their children away from London, ours definitely would as well. Just when I thought the lunch bell would never sound, the first clang was heard and we all squirmed in our seats. Eventually Mr. Blake wound up his discussion, the lunch session had begun.

On sunny days David and I usually make a mad dash for the schoolyard. Unfortunately, today the weather had changed and the bright sunny morning had given way to a cloudy afternoon with rain clouds on the horizon. This meant that lunch would be enjoyed inside at our desks.

Before I even opened my lunch bag, I leaned over to David.

"David, thanks."

That was all I could get out before Billy and Albert walked over.

"*Blimey*, David, why didn't you tell the whole story to everyone?" Billy asked.

"What for?" David answered.

"Well, you're a proper hero," Albert said.

"No. I only did what I had to. There was no bravery involved."

David opened the paper that covered his sandwich and did not waste any time devouring it. There were more important issues at the moment, and eating was one of them.

"Peter didn't even try to help, but you did it right away," Albert persisted.

"Yeah, well I needed the money more than Peter. OK? Let it drop!"

David had raised his voice and several other children looked our way. He went back to finishing his sandwich and it finally dawned on Billy and Albert that the subject was closed.

"David, you really are a hero," I said to him

The others had drifted away. He needed to know how I felt, even if he didn't want to hear it from them he had to hear it from me.

"Listen, *mate*, going into a hole for a *shilling* doesn't make me a hero."

"As far as I'm concerned it does. I'd not have done it for all the jewels in the king's crown."

He tapped me kindly on my head and reached over for my lunch.

"I'm starving. Can I have half of your sandwich?"

"Here, have it all. You deserve it!"

"Thanks! Cheese and cucumber, yummy."

David scoffed down the sandwich as I bit into my apple. We sat looking out the window when a thunder cloud broke over the school. It violently vibrated the windows, and for a second I thought we were under attack. My body began to shake involuntarily.

"*Blimey*! That felt like a bomb!" I said.

"No. Dad said Hitler isn't going to be sending planes over in the daylight to hit London. It's too risky for them," David assured me.

The rain came down in torrents beating heavily against the window panes. Lightning flashed in the distance, and the sound of thunder would soon be heard. When the thunder did sound, I was ready for it and rather than jumping in fear, I went to the window. Rushing down the roads, the rain water was taking much of the debris caused by the bombing along with it. If this weather continued, the streets would be cleaned, but the bombed buildings would be drenched leaving anything that had survived to be destroyed by the downfall. Even nature was fighting us.

When Doreen joined us at the window, David instantly turned a shade of bright pink. It appeared that lately both of us were having difficulty keeping our composure around her, but she didn't notice.

"What do you two think about Bess and Grace going to Scotland?" she asked.

"I didn't know they had family up there. Probably the best thing for those two. They were terrified to wear their gas masks. They both said they couldn't breathe with them on," David said.

"The masks are very uncomfortable to wear, but do you think that was the reason?" I asked.

"No, I think their parents decided it was too dangerous for them to stay in London. Even my parents are thinking that way. Not much we can do about it when adults make decisions for us," Doreen replied.

"Are your parents going to send you away again, Doe?" David asked.

"Yes, my mother has decided that all of us are going to stay with my Granny until this stops," she answered.

"What about your father, is he going as well?" I said.

"Oh no! Since Daddy is a doctor at St. Bartholomew's Hospital, he can't possibly get away. He's needed to help with all the casualties that come in during the attacks."

"Wow, he must see some pretty horrible things," David blurted out.

"Yes, I am sure he does, but he never talks about them to us. I imagine he thinks it will make us ill. But we read the papers and even see things on the streets, so I really don't know why he feels he must protect us."

She was so matter of fact that I wondered if she had aspirations to follow in her father's footsteps.

"Would you like to be a doctor one day, Doe?" I asked.

"Yes, I want to be a surgeon, but Daddy says women aren't accepted in that area of medicine. I told him things are changing very quickly, and even that attitude will change."

"You're right. If this war continues, more men will be called up to fight, and already women are doing men's work," I rationalized.

Before she could respond, Mr. Blake returned to the classroom, and we took our seats again. The afternoon lessons had been shortened since the *Blitz* had begun, since the objective was for us all to return home before any bombing might begin. The day would be over soon, but in the meantime, I listened to the monotonous voices reciting various poems and was thankful I hadn't been called upon.

When I looked over at David I saw that his eyes were slits and his head kept bobbing downward onto his chest. He had fallen asleep. Several other students were having difficulty remaining awake, and I wondered why Mr. Blake had not reprimanded them until I noticed even his eyes were shut. His lips were puckered, and a stream of air must have been blowing from them because I could hear him snoring ever so lightly.

We were all exhausted from the past nights' successive bombings, even my eyes glazed over and soon I was in that cloudy state between sleep and wakefulness, when the last bells for dismissal rang. David jumped up in a dither, and Mr. Blake was so startled he almost fell off his chair. It was impossible not to chuckle at the sight.

David was rubbing his eyes and yawning. He apparently had been in a deep sleep.

"*Blimey*! I was having a wonderful dream about baked ham and mince pie when the bell rang," David said.

The rain had temporarily stopped, and we walked out of the school into a dull afternoon. We started our trek home when Doreen called over to us, so we waited for her. She appeared excited about something and was in a hurry to share it with us.

"Listen, I have a wonderful idea. Why don't you two come and visit me when I'm in Princes Risborough? You could take the train up, and even stay for a long weekend. Granny has plenty of room."

The idea was terrific, and I was about to agree that it would be great fun when I realized I could not make any plans. I was being sent away in several days. Apparently, David had the same thoughts and was first to speak.

"Doe that sounds wonderful, but we both have one tiny problem," he said.

"Yes, Doe, it does sound wonderful, unfortunately David and I might be sent away as well. I'm likely going north again to my Auntie Nan's in Carlisle, and David's parents are thinking of having him go to his sister's in Ireland."

"What! You two never told me! When did this happen? How could you keep this from me? I thought we were pals?"

"Hold on, Doe, we just learned this last night. Peter's dad and my mum decided this during the attack last night. It shocked us too." David tried to calm her, but it didn't work.

"How long will you both be away? Ireland is so far away, and as for Carlisle, you might as well be in Iceland," she moaned.

"Come on, Doe, it won't be so bad. We'll write just like we did last time."

I now tried a different tactic; however, she wasn't making things easy for me. I didn't want to go, but as David had pointed out, we had no choice.

"It's just that I never thought this would happen. I hate this war! Write! David hardly ever wrote!" Doreen wailed.

"None of us like it, do you think I like hiding under the stairs when those *Heinkels* start dropping explosives on us? And although Peter is terrified to go into the Anderson shelter, I think he's even more afraid to go up north," David announced.

I could not believe my ears. I felt my face turning red, and my ears burning. What was David thinking? Suddenly he looked at me and realized what he had said. He clapped his hand over his mouth, rolled his eyes around in their sockets and lowered his head.

Doe looked at David and then turned to me.

"Whatever is he talking about? Why have you been keeping this from me? You're afraid to go into the shelter? Is this because you were trapped in it when you tried to prove you were brilliant? And why are you afraid to go up north? I don't believe this. Peter, talk to me," Doe demanded.

"What am I supposed to say? Thanks, David," I shouted at him.

"Peter, stop acting this way. It's Doe, she's a pal. Besides everyone at school knew the shelter collapsed under you. Remember you were out of school for two weeks with that concussion. Something like that was news that spread around the school in a day. Don't be so *daft*!" David hollered at me.

"And it would make perfect sense that because you had such a horrible accident you would naturally be afraid to go into it afterwards. But what's this about going north?" Doe persisted.

"Ask him, he seems to know everything!" I screamed this at her while pointing to David.

"Peter, whatever has gotten into you? I understand how you must feel about this war and the consequences of it. We both do," she said.

"No, you don't know how I feel. Neither of you know how I feel."

I turned my back to them and began to walk home. David called to me, but I kept walking. I wanted nothing to do with him. He was supposed to be my best *mate* and he told Doe my secret!

Chapter Twelve

I walked quickly, and at times broke into a run. My intent was to get home as fast as possible, so I didn't pay attention to the neighborhoods I passed through, after all, I had witnessed the *Blitz*'s damage in the morning. There was no need to experience it again. All I wanted to do was to reach home and shut myself in my room. I had been betrayed. Sure, Doe is a pal, but I didn't want her to know what a coward she has for a friend. Nothing mattered any more.

My mind was spinning and when I pushed the garden gate open Toffee's welcoming barking stopped the whirlwind in my head. She stood in front of me and continued barking until I acknowledged her.

"Hello, Toffee, have you been a good girl today?"

She ran several circles around me preventing me from taking another step forward until I gave her one of her doggie treats which I always carried in my pocket. I reached in, and pulled one out. Seeing this she immediately sat down and raised her front paws up in a gesture of begging, a trick I had taught her as a puppy. I gave her the treat which she wolfed down in one bite. Satisfied she ran into the open kitchen door. I followed her into the house, and was stopped by the unexpected scene in the kitchen.

Mum was talking with Tillie who was home from work at an extraordinarily early hour. Their conversation stopped when I entered the house, something was up.

"Mum, Tillie is everything okay?" I asked fearing the worst.

"Oh Peter, things are definitely brewing," Tillie answered.

"Would you like a cup of tea, Peter?" Mum asked as she poured cups for herself and my sister.

It has always been said that the English solve all problems with a cup-o-tea, and this obviously was one of those times. Something definitely was brewing besides the tea, and my curiosity surpassed my need to sulk in my room.

"Thanks, Mum, I'd like that. Do you have any *biscuits* to go with my tea, I'm famished,"

"Didn't you eat your lunch?" she asked.

There are times in my life when I have realized it is better to tell a little white lie than to divulge the truth which would require a great deal of explaining. How could I tell her David ate my sandwich without an explanation?

"Oh, yes, the apple was delicious."

I answered her, and was glad that what I had told her was exactly the truth.

Mum brought out a tin of *biscuits,* and poured me a cup of tea. I watched the steam rise in tiny swirls above the cup and reached for a ginger snap *biscuit.*

Both Tillie and Mum watched me as I carefully poured a spoonful of sugar into the cup and added a little milk. Their attention was a little unnerving, so I finally got up the courage to question.

"Tillie, you're home rather early. Anything happen?"

At this Tillie's blue eyes flashed. She jumped up from her chair, and became extremely animated.

"Peter, Madame Gina is closing the shop."

"Closing the shop? Why's she doing that?" I asked.

Tillie struck a pose and in an exaggerated French accent, imitated Madame Gina's explanation.

"Because women aren't buying ze fancy dresses now ze war is on. It is impossible to buy silk. It all goes to ze making of parachutes. To obtain cotton is impossible, since it must be imported. Ze only fabric we can get is wool. Sheep are plentiful and their wool can be spun into yarn for ze looms. But even that is limited, since making ze wool is *nécessaire* to make the military men's uniforms."

I had to laugh at Tillie's imitation of her boss. Tillie caught her breath and continued on in her own voice.

"We have hundreds of bolts of cloth and I think Madame Gina is using all this as an excuse."

"Then what do you think is the real reason?" I asked.

"She's afraid of the shop being bombed and losing everything," Tillie answered.

"I believe you're right, Tillie. That is definitely her real reason for closing her shop. Who can blame her?" Mum said.

"Madame Gina has made inquiries and taken a lease on a shop in Oxford," Tillie explained.

"But won't ladies not buy fancy dresses there as well?" I questioned her.

"Ah, there's a difference. In Oxford, the shop will specialize in everyday items, and in a university town, professors' wives and children will always need clothes. Madame Gina is a very smart business woman."

Madame Gina had made a small tailor's shop into a fashionable ladies' boutique attracting women from all over London to shop for their gowns and dressy outfits at her shop. Tillie loved working there. Tillie's face beamed, it was obvious there was still more to the story.

"Madame Gina has asked me to go to Oxford with her and be the manageress of the shop. This is a marvelous opportunity, and I intend to learn as much as possible from her. Closing the shop in London has turned around to my benefit."

I was not ready for what she said next.

"This means that I'm to leave London and live in Oxford!"

My mother obviously agreed this was a good move because her next words stunned me.

"This is really wonderful, Tillie. You will be safer in Oxford and Madame Gina will love having you with her. You are her favorite."

I could not believe what I'd just heard. Tillie's life had taken a dramatic turn in a short period of time, and so had mine.

"When is this going to happen?" I asked.

"Immediately, we started packing up the goods today and by the end of the week everything is being shipped out to Oxford. I must go up and start packing my things so I can leave with Madame Gina on the weekend."

"But where will you live? You can't just run up to Oxford without *digs*."

"No problem, Madame Gina has procured a flat with two bedrooms and I'm to stay with her until I've a place of my own. She doesn't care how long I stay with her. Isn't it marvelous?"

It was all planned. Tillie was leaving me. Who will I snuggle against in the shelter? Who will tell stories to help me get through the nights? How will I survive the *Blitz* without her?

My tea had grown cold, and the *biscuits* I had eaten felt like lead in my stomach. Today was proving to be the worst day of my life. Little did I know that more disturbing news was about to arrive.

My sister ran up the stairs, and I could hear her moving about in her room as she opened her wardrobe door and dresser drawers. She wasn't wasting anytime time preparing for her departure. I wondered what Daddy would think of all this when he arrived home. I slowly climbed the stairs and peeked into Tillie's room where clothes were strewn on her bed, shoes lined up next to it, and an old valise open on the floor. Humming a popular song, it was obvious that Tillie was happy in her decision. I had a feeling she wasn't even thinking about me as she whirled about collecting whatever personal items she chose to pack.

I went into my room, slammed the door and flopped on my bed. For the past hour I had forgotten what occurred at school, but now the recollection overwhelmed me. Should I wait for David at our spot tomorrow morning? Should I act as though nothing happened? How was I going to face Doreen? Try as I might I couldn't just get these thoughts out of my mind. Hoping I could dispel them with work, I opened my math book, but the numbers meant nothing to me, it was impossible to think.

An idea began to slowly materialize, maybe when the next attack occurred if I proved I was brave enough to enter the shelter without being afraid, my parents wouldn't send me to my aunt's. Then I could tell David and Doe the reason I was staying and everything would be forgotten. While this seemed like a good idea, the mere thought of being in the shelter caused me to feel cold all over, and with Tillie gone, it would be even harder to put up a good show. However, will I manage without her?

I heard Toffee barking and knew that my father had arrived home.

Obviously intent on telling him her news right away, Tillie was already out of her room and running down the stairs. I decided not to go down and instead listened at the top of the stairs as Tillie's excited voice carried up to me. My father was quiet throughout her entire monologue, until she asked him his opinion.

"Well, Daddy, what do you think?"

"I think this idea of Madame Gina has merit. You'll be safer in Oxford. If she wants to take you with her, by all means go."

Daddy sounded happy and I wondered if he was pleased that at least one of his children had the sense to leave London. Tillie let out a squeal of delight, and was about to run back upstairs when Daddy asked her to stay. His voice had taken on a different tone and something warned me that a dark cloud was going to settle over us.

"Peter, please come down. I need to talk to you."

"Right-o, Daddy."

I tried to sound as though all was wonderful in my world, but I really was very frightened. What was going to happen now? Had he contacted Auntie Nan? Was I being shipped out earlier?

"Peter, thank you for coming down. Margaret, Tillie, I have something to say that will affect all of us."

"George, what is it?"

Fear registered in my mother's face. Tillie had turned very quiet and we all waited for my father to continue speaking. "We are going to have to send Toffee away."

I had not expected this. My mother looked stunned and Tillie responded as though she did not quite understand what Daddy had said. "Send Toffee away, whatever are you talking about, Daddy?"

Daddy was holding the spaniel and rubbing her long silky ears very gently. He didn't look up at us, his eyes remained fixed on Toffee. Her big brown eyes gazed up at him lovingly.

"There has been a recommendation made that owners of cats and dogs are to send their pets away. The nightly bombing is causing the animals too much stress. You all see how Toffee shakes when we are attacked. It's terribly unfair to her. Even during the day, the slightest noise upsets her. It is the humane thing to do."

"Send her away, but where?" Mum asked.

"Maybe I can take her with me to Oxford. Madame Gina loves Toffee," Tillie suggested.

"No, I don't think that is a good idea. It will be difficult enough for you and Madame Gina getting things set up. She most certainly doesn't need a dog around to confuse things," Daddy said.

I'd been listening to this conversation in disbelief. Once again everyone was talking about something that concerned me as though I wasn't in the room. It was my time to speak up.

"I won't do it! Toffee is my dog. Call me selfish, but I refuse to do it!"

Although, my voice was shaky, I was in control of my emotions and spoke out with tremendous conviction. I definitely got my parents' attention. Daddy shook his head, and Mummy raised her hand to her mouth.

I had no solution at the moment. If I said that I'd take Toffee with me to Auntie Nan's then I had basically agreed to go north, and this was a battle I was still fighting. I didn't wait for them to respond. I walked over to my father, removed Toffee from his hold and grasped her tightly in my arms. She nuzzled me and licked my face. I stroked her shiny coat and gently blew into her face. This war was asking me to make too many sacrifices, but no one was going to separate Toffee from me! I had done it once when I went to Auntie Nan's. I wouldn't do it again. Carrying my dog, I turned and went up to my room. I lowered Toffee gently onto the bed and continued petting her until she settled down next to me.

On my seventh birthday Mum and Dad brought me to a neighbor whose spaniel had puppies. I was ecstatic when my parents told me I could choose one. When I bent over the pen to play with them the runt of the litter crawled over to me and licked my fingers. I immediately chose her over all the others. I named her Toffee because she was the color of butterscotch toffee. As she grew older her coloring darkened, but her coat still shone in the sunlight. She always sensed my moods. When I was happy she frolicked around with me, and when I was miserable she'd somehow comforted me. I had to admit that Toffee has been shaken by the nightly attacks, but I could not part with her. Not again!

Was it really important that Doe knew I couldn't decide whether I hated being in the shelter more than going north? Did I really care if David often spoke without thinking? These things suddenly seemed trivial compared to loosing Toffee. Tomorrow I decided I would act as though nothing had happened and even laugh if the subject came up.

"Blimey! Toffee, this is a very grown up attitude," I said to her.

Toffee had been watching me from under half shut eyes. When she heard her name, she lifted her head and tilted it from left to right. I reached over and fondled her floppy ears.

"You're my good girl. Don't you worry no one is going to send you away."

She settled down and within seconds was asleep. I would have loved to join her and get some sleep but I had to attack my homework before supper. Now that I had made my decision, I concentrated on the equations and hurried through the assignment without any difficulty. I had just finished when Mum called me for supper. At the kitchen table, I expected to hear more of the plan to send pets away, but apparently someone had given the order that the subject of Toffee not be discussed. Instead as we ate our meal Tillie's move to Oxford was the subject of conversation.

Tillie and Mum were wondering what to pack, when Daddy reminded them both that Oxford wasn't that far away and we could post anything she might forget. It felt odd how everyone was behaving, especially after my outburst.

After supper Mummy pulled down the blackout shades, and Daddy turned on the *wireless*. The commentator was advising the listeners that we should all take our prime minister's advice to heart.

He was especially reminding us that in June, Mr. Churchill had addressed the House of Commons where he said the British people had to "*brace ourselves to our duties,*" and that years to come people would say, "*This was their finest hour.*"

This statement puzzled me, how could we possibly brace ourselves to our duties when the enemy controlled our nights? As for people one day saying it was our finest hour, that was *crackers*! I left Daddy in the parlor as he listened to the news, and went upstairs. I needed to concentrate on an English assignment, to memorize a poem, and I hadn't even chosen one.

I searched through the poetry book, but all the poems were a bit soppy and didn't appeal to me at all. Then I found one that didn't go on about lost love, and put my mind to memorizing it. After about an hour, I decided I had enough.

Preparing for bed, I placed both shoes next to the chair where my robe and gas mask were slung. I took my extra blanket and folded it on the seat of the chair. Tonight, when the sirens sounded, I was ready for the shelter.

Earlier I had pulled down the blackout shades. Now before getting into bed I snuck a look out the window. Normally with all the street lights out and the houses' windows blackened it was quite dark. But tonight, a dense fog had drifted in over the city, making it even more impossible to see anything beyond the window pane. Hopefully the fog would protect us from our attackers.

Toffee was already fast asleep at the foot of my bed, and didn't even move when I climbed into it. I pulled the covers up to my chin, shouted good night to everyone who one by one answered me. Suddenly I was very sleepy.

I was just drifting off to sleep when I heard voices on the stairs' landing. Mum and Dad. were discussing me, so I lifted my head from the pillow and listened carefully.

"I sent a telegram to Nan and asked if we could send Peter back to her," Daddy said.

"How long did you say he was to stay?" Mum asked him.

"Fact is I didn't. First things first. This time I think you should go up with him and stay for a few days."

"That's a splendid idea, and perhaps while I'm up there I can learn why he despised the idea of being there. I really don't think it had anything to do with leaving us, no matter what he said. What do you think, George?"

"Yes, Margaret, something else is bothering him, and then there's the problem with Toffee. We've got to sort this out."

Down the hall their bedroom door closed, and their conversation was silenced, but what little I heard told me one thing was for sure, Daddy was determined not to waste any time in sending me north. The thought of going north, and living in daily fear of Colin was unbearable, but there was one consolation, if I was forced to go, I'd take Toffee. I rolled over onto my side, punched the pillow and settled down, Toffee moved and curled up at my feet. Her warmth relaxed me.

Maybe tonight I'll get the opportunity to show my change of heart from a cowardly one to a brave one, like the lion going off to Oz.

Chapter Thirteen

There hadn't been a raid, and I actually slept in my own bed for the entire night. What joy, but unfortunately the privilege of sleeping in my own bed came with consequences. I was unable to prove my bravery to my father, yet in reality, I was rather glad I didn't have to spend the night in the horrid shelter.

The fog had lifted, and the day was starting out to be a clear one. I took this as a good omen, and dressed quickly. Once downstairs I gobbled down my breakfast, and hurried out to school. My father and Tillie had left for work while Mum was already in the garden. Yesterday's rain had washed the silt and dust off all her flowers and veggies, and she was busy surveying them.

"Any damage done, Mum?" I asked on my way out the gate.

"Except for the roses which are so fragile, everything appears fine."

I picked up a stick and sent it flying through the garden for Toffee to retrieve. She bounded after it and seconds later was at my feet where she dropped her quarry. Her mouth lolled open and her little rump swung back and forth.

"What a clever girl you are, Toffee. Here's your treat."

Within seconds she devoured it. I stroked her and started off to school.

My mother called after me.

"Have a splendid day, Peter."

"That's what I intend to do, Mum, bye."

My decision to disregard all that I had said yesterday to David and Doe elated me this morning. I wanted to get to the meeting place early and surprise David. I hurried along at my fastest pace. Today the roads were full of lorries and workmen. Broken windows were being boarded up, charred walls were being torn down, and rubbish was being loaded away. There was a general air of relief, for we had been spared one night of bombing.

I picked up my speed and broke into a run, and was almost at our appointed meeting place. This would be a shocker for David. But the surprise was on me, because walking away from our rendezvous were both David and Doreen!

"Blimey! Look who's coming our way, Doe," David said spitefully.

"Looks like that fellow who was a friend of ours. You know that Peter Morris," Doe answered unpleasantly.

"Hello you two, didn't expect to see you here."

I said this all the while trying to ignore the nasty tones to their voices.

"I bet you didn't," Doe replied sharply.

She turned her back to me and kept walking.

David remained at her side, and whispered to her. She looked over her shoulder at me, and gave me a cold look. This was not going as I had planned, what was wrong? Had I hurt them so much? Didn't they realize they had upset me? I had to talk to them before we got to school, but I suspected they were not going to listen to me. I had to give it a go.

With their heads held high, they continued talking to each other and kept walking as though I hadn't said a word. David and Doe weren't interested in anything I had to say. My foolish pride had made me lose my best *mate* and closest pal, because my plan had failed.

I hung back and sadly watched them hurry along toward school. Soon they disappeared through the school doors.

Billy and Albert came up the road to my right and began snickering.

"Been in any rabbit holes lately, David?" Albert shouted to me.

Billy slapped him on the shoulder.

"That's a good one, Albert."

They both laughed at my expense and sauntered along toward school. I wanted to respond, but couldn't think of anything to shout in retaliation. I was crushed.

I walked into the classroom, found my seat and busied myself with my books and homework. Mr. Blake had obviously been in the classroom for several minutes because the black board was full of math problems, the school day had begun.

Unlike yesterday, when we bowed our heads in silent prayer I did not feel too magnanimous toward my fellow man. Nor did I feel the surge of patriotism that I had yesterday when singing. I tried to concentrate on the lesson, but again like yesterday had no success. Yesterday I was concerned that my parents would send me north, and I would have to face Colin. Today I felt it was even worst here in London where I had to face David and Doreen. If only we had never gotten that blasted Anderson shelter! If only I hadn't been so smug, and tried to complete the job myself! If only I had stood up against Colin! If only! If only! But it had happened, and I had to face the results of my actions.

The day had turned warm, the windows had been pushed open, and a soft breeze coming through the window rustled the pages on our desks. I stared out the window and looked beyond the schoolyard. From this viewpoint, the church steeple rose at an odd angle, because it had been hit during the recent bombing.

My mind wandered to the sights we had encountered yesterday morning. I wondered how the little girl with the *pram* was this morning. Had her mother been killed? This morning we awoke, did others? Mr. Blake's voice interrupted my reverie.

"Ladies and gentlemen, I sincerely hope that each of you selected a poem of your liking from your book of poems. Mr. Morris, would you please recite the poem you chose?"

I rose from my chair, cleared my throat.

"O, to be in England
Now that April 's there,
And whoever wakes in England
Survives*, some morning, unaware,*
*That the lowest **bombs** and the brushwood sheaf.."*

Several girls started giggling, and many of the boys let out low hoots. Mr. Blake looked at me strangely. I had made a terrible blunder!

I had substituted Browning's words with those from my thoughts. I began again.

"O, to be..."

My words were drowned by the blare of the air raid sirens. The Nazis were flying across the channel to attack London in broad daylight! Our voices rose in disbelief. Mr. Blake shouted above us.

"Everyone, grab your gas masks and process out the room immediately. Make your way out of the school and into our assigned shelter. Let's not waste time. Get a move on!"

We filed out and rushed down the hall. Students and teachers were emerging from all the rooms and running out the building. Before I reached the doors, I realized I was carrying my book bag and not my gas mask. I had to get my mask! I turned and tried pushing my way back through the crowds of exiting children. The throng of students made it impossible to make my way through the main hall. I turned and took another route. I had just gone around the corner when I heard shrill crying coming from one of the rooms. It was the nursery.

I pushed the door open, and was totally unprepared for what I found. The nursery was in a complete uproar. The little children were beside themselves. They were totally out of control and carrying on hysterically. Their teacher was not in the room! A little red-haired girl was hiding under the teacher's desk. A bigger boy had crawled in after her, and was trying unsuccessfully to pull her out. Standing on a chair, a small blond boy waved his arms about and shouted incoherently. Several children were running around in circles. While others sat on the floor, covered their ears and moaned pathetically. They had no idea what was happening, and panic registered on all their small faces. I had to act fast.

"Come here, love, I'll take care of you," I said ever so gently.

I reached for her under the desk. She crawled out, followed by her would-be rescuer. I hoisted the girl onto my shoulders and tightly grabbed the boy's hand. Then I shouted above the noise.

"Children, all of you, calm down immediately!"

Instantly twenty some odd little faces looked up at me. The crying quieted down to whimpering. The small blond boy jumped down from his chair, while those who had been running around stopped, and the children who had been on the floor stood up. I had their attention, especially since I was in control of two of their classmates.

"Now everyone, I am Peter, and I am your leader. You are all to follow what I tell you, because we are going to play a game. First, I want all of you to quickly get your gas masks, and hang them around your necks."

The children immediately ran to the hooks on the wall, pulled down their masks and followed my direction. The little blond boy ran up to me with three extra masks in his hands. He pointed at the red-haired girl on my shoulders and the boy at my side.

"These are for Jenny and Ian, and this big one is for you," he said in a high-pitched voice.

"Thank you, young man," I said, and handed Jenny and Ian their masks.

Then I shouted loudly to get the children's attention again.

"Now I want you to hold hands. We are going to make a long line like a centipede. You are all to follow after me as fast as a centipede scurries across a wall. Are you ready?"

A murmur of agreement rumbled through the room. They quickly reached for one another's hands. Once I saw that each child had another's hand, we started out the door and through the hall. I still held Jenny on my shoulders and Ian by the hand. The halls were now empty, and it was easier to guide my charges through the school. I kept turning my head to check that I had all of them with me. This was a bit difficult except for the fact that the blond boy had decided to be the tail end of the centipede, so I had a good reference point. Besides, I suspected that if anyone dropped from the line he would let me know.

We dashed out the building and into the empty schoolyard. Everyone was in the shelters. The sound of the sirens was deafening. In the distance, I heard the rumbling of explosives, and the whirling of aircraft. The children tagged along after me as we darted behind the school toward the long shelters. I saw the door of the furthest shelter gaping open, and I hurried the children toward it. Luckily it was empty. I thought of what Mr. Churchill had said recently,

"We must brace ourselves to our duties..."

Taking care of these children was my duty, and I had to brace myself to it at all costs!

I pushed the door open wider to begin the process of getting them into safety. I tried to take Jenny off my shoulders, but she desperately hung onto me. Ian looked up at me and I nodded to him.

"That's a good lad, Ian. You be the first to go in, show your friends how brave you are."

Ian smiled and entered. From the rear of the line, Blondie ran forward and followed his friend. He shouted wildly and ran to the back of the structure. One by one the children ran into the safety of the shelter until the last child, a tiny green-eyed girl, stopped at the entrance and refused to go in.

"I can'na go in," she cried.

"What's your name, love?" I asked hoping to gain her confidence.

"Lucy," she answered between her pitiful sobs.

"Well, Lucy, all your friends are in there now. And Jenny and I will be going in too." I told her comfortingly.

"But you see, I'm afraid of the dark, an' it's very dark in there."

What could I say to this child? I looked into her green eyes, saw the horror she was experiencing, and I understood. How could I ask this child to face her fright when I was unable to face my own? I looked into the dark ominous interior of the vast metal shelter.

The thunderous blasts of nearby bombs were deafening, The Nazis were flying toward us and getting closer with each second, we had no choice. By hesitating outside the shelter, we were endangering the welfare of all the children, just as every night when I hesitated, I had put my own family in peril. What a fool I had been.

"Lucy, I can't leave you outside alone. You must go in. I promise I'll protect you. Let's go, Lucy."

I touched her hand and she allowed me to hold it in mine. Her tears stained her face, but her crying had stopped. With Jenny on my shoulders I led Lucy into the shelter. As I secured the heavy metal door, an enemy escort fighter plane swooped overhead. Behind it would be the *Henkel* with its cargo of explosives.

"Jenny, you must get off my shoulders now. I can't stand straight in here."

This obvious statement successfully persuaded Jenny to release her hold on me and clamber down, only to sit on my feet. Apparently, she felt secure as long as she was on one end of me. Meanwhile Lucy looked terribly pathetic standing in front of me. I picked her up and placed her on my lap. She rested her curly head against my chest and I could feel her trembling. This made me think momentarily of Toffee and I hoped the spaniel was safe with Mum in our shelter. I didn't allow myself to dwell too long on this. My thoughts switched to Tillie and Dad and prayed they had taken cover in the Underground.

My palms began to sweat, but I felt a chill. I blinked my eyes several times to become accustomed to the dim light from a couple of *torches* two children had found and switched on. The walls of the shelter shut in on me. I breathed laboriously. Any minute now I would feel the all too familiar waves of nausea. I waited.

Bombs fell. Planes flew above us. My breathing slowed down. I did not feel cold. When I looked down, my palms they were no longer damp. I stared deep into the shelter and was astonished. The anxiety I encountered whenever I stayed in the shelter was still there, but it was not overwhelming me. I was controlling it! I was controlling the lives of these children!

Chapter Fourteen

The children sat patiently on the benches lining each side of the shelter. Occasionally one of them began to sniffle, or even whimper very quietly. These poor little things needed encouragement to survive this nightmare.

"What a splendid job you all did. I am very proud of you, and I think it would be nice if I learned each of your names."

From deep inside the shelter a familiar voice piped up.

"My name is Rodney, Sir."

This came from the little blond boy who had kindly retrieved the gas masks for his classmates and me.

"Very good, Rodney. Now what about you?"

When I turned to the child on my left, I realized Ian was sitting next to me. He looked at me with a blank stare, and then occupied himself with his gas mask.

"Oh, Sir, you remember, his name is Ian. And Sir, he doesn't speak," volunteered Rodney.

"Thank you for that bit of information, Rodney."

After this exchange, the children each told me their names.

Rodney shouted to me from his spot in the rear of the shelter.

"Sir, are we going to wait in the tunnel until a train arrives?"

Rodney's strange question made immediate sense to me. This child's family was one of the many who found shelter in the Underground. Obviously, he had never been in a shelter of this kind.

"Well, Rodney, we may have to wait a very long time, because trains don't come in here."

His happy disposition made me more aware that it was my responsibility to transform this horrific experience for the rest of them.

"I have an idea, why don't we all sing a jolly song?"

"Peter, I would like that," Lucy said to me.

"Yes, let's sing *Old MacDonald's Farm*, Peter, Sir." Jenny begged from her position on my feet.

"I think that is a wonderful idea! Everyone now, let's start!"

Old MacDonald had a farm, E-I-E-I-O
And on his farm, he had a cow, E-I-E-I-O
With a moo-moo here and a moo-moo there
Here a moo there a moo
Everywhere a moo-moo
Old MacDonald had a farm, E-I-E-I-O

Most of the children raised their voices, but a few remained silent. I prompted them to join in the fun. After a little cajoling they did, except for Ian who remained silent, and was obviously content to listen.

Inside the shelter it sounded as though a party was in progress, but outside the sounds told the truth. A war was being fought and we were the target. Several explosions occurred so near to the shelter that with each one the entire structure shook violently. After a particularly close bombardment, I heard a child cry out followed by the shouts of others demanding my attention. The singing stopped abruptly, and after I managed to have Lucy and Jenny separate their hold on me, I rushed to investigate what had happened deep within the shelter.

The explosion had loosened a wooden pinning from the ceiling. It had hit Rodney! He had fallen onto the wooden plank floor, and lay very still. Blood colored the flaxen hair on his forehead a bright red. Kneeling over him, I feared the worst.

"Rodney, can you hear me? Rodney, can you open your eyes?"

"Rodney, Rodney, please wake up!" This plea came from an unexpected source, Ian.

I gently rested my hand on Rodney's chest. His chest was moving up and down. He was alive!

"Rodney, Rodney, come on lad, open your eyes for Ian. He's calling to you," I said, but this time with more confidence.

"Ian, ask your friend to wake up again. Would you please?"

The child nodded, and this time his voice was louder and clearer as it bounced off the steel walls, and filled the shelter.

"RODNEY, STOP SLEEPING. WAKE UP!!"

The fallen boy's nose twitched, his eyes blinked, and a slow wide smile grew on his thin little face.

"Hello, is that you, Ian?" he impishly asked.

The children had been watching silently in apprehension. Now they let out a loud cheer, their friend was awoken, and for them this meant he was fine. I cradled his little head in my lap and looked at his wound. There was a nasty gash on his forehead, bleeding heavily. I removed my shirt which caused a certain amount of oohing and ahhing among the children, especially the little girls, and tore it to pieces. Inwardly I laughed to myself, and wondered what they were imagining. I applied pressure to the wound and hoped for the best.

"Rodney, how do you feel, old chap?"

"Sir, I feel like a ton of coal fell upon me."

"Very well described. Do you think you can sit up for me and rest against Ian's legs if he is right here behind you?"

Ian had taken a place on the bench directly beside me. He was ready to serve his friend however he needed. He nodded his head in agreement and motioned to Rodney to sit in front of him.

"Yes, sir, I believe I can do that. Ian, are you really speaking now?" Rodney asked in amazement.

"Course it's me speaking. I never spoke cause I never 'ad anything important to say, Rod," Ian replied.

This answer caused several of the children to giggle, while others didn't understand the logic of his statement. When Rodney leaned his back against Ian's legs it occurred to me that Ian was only five years old. How could I ask him to apply pressure to Rodney's head, and possibly get his hands bloody in the act? But I had to, because I was concerned that I must be available for any further emergency.

"Ian, I am going to ask you to do something very grown up. Do you think you can hold this cloth against Rodney's head to stop the bleeding? Your hands may get blood on them."

"Sir, for Rodney I'll do it. Don't 'cha worry, Sir."

Ian gazed down at Rodney with great devotion. The boys gave each other a look that reminded me of the many David and I had exchanged in hard times. Ian and Rodney were destined to become the greatest of friends.

I moved toward the entrance of the shelter when an exceptionally loud explosion rocked us. Small particles of cement streamed down. Several children fell from the benches, and immediately began to howl. Those remaining seated were visibly upset. I immediately walked between the benches, and gave each child a pat and some encouragement. I helped those who had fallen to their seats again, and checked on Rodney who was resting comfortably against Ian's boney knees.

"What brave little soldiers you all are. Tell me children, shall we continue our song?"

I hoped they would respond in the affirmative, and was not disappointed. This time Lucy surprised me. Her tiny little voice screamed out the first verses which vibrated off the walls. The others followed her lead. They were mooing and clucking and heehawing to their hearts content. Above them the attack ravaged on, and silently I prayed we would make it out of this without any further casualties.

I did not want them to lose interest in the activity, so I introduced another bit to the game.

"Now, listen very carefully to what you are to do next," I told them above the noise outside.

All eyes fixed on me, their leader, and I would not disappoint them.

"When you sing out an animal's name you are to move like the animal. For example, as you sing about Old MacDonald's goose, flap your arms like one. Just watch me. Can you do it?"

They were excited over this new aspect to the singing. Within minutes, I had them trying to wiggle their ears like donkeys, and twitch their noses like rabbits. They successfully pecked their little heads up and down like chickens, and squirmed about like pigs. They shook their heads like ponies, and cleaned their faces like cats, but they lost their composure when I shook my bottom like a puppy. Instantly they were shaking their little *bums* and laughing outrageously, as they continued singing and acting out. I had succeeded in dispelling their fears, and even my own. This was indeed a triumph! We were so busy squawking and flapping, barking and shaking, meowing and oinking that we did not hear the all clear sirens.

It was Rodney who shouted so loudly that he alarmed Ian.

"Sir, Sir, we can leave. Listen there's the signal!"

I raised my hand to silence the children, and we listened quietly. The noise of planes and bombs had stopped and now the only sound we heard was the all clear signal. The children started hooraying and jumping up and down excitedly. I had to gain control.

"Children, remember I am the leader. Let's become a centipede again. Take the hand of the friend you came in with. Girls, I must carry Rodney out. Ian, you come here with Jenny and Lucy, and each of you take one of Ian's hands. Ian, you be the first to follow me out with Jenny and Lucy. Then, children, you all follow us!"

I stooped down. Although the bleeding had subsided slightly, Rodney's face was very pale, but he managed to give me a crooked smile. I fashioned a bandage from my remaining torn shirt, wrapped it around his head, and very carefully lifted him up into my arms.

"You are a brave lad, Rodney"

"Thank you, Sir. Are you sure no trains come through here?"

"Quite sure, Rodney." I told him.

I slowly pushed open the scarred door with my back, and led the children out. The scene outside was one of complete chaos. Smoke filled the autumn air. The school had taken a direct hit. Flames were shooting through the windows. Glass was bursting and flying about. Firemen were trying to extinguish the blaze. Several trees were cracked in two and lay in pieces about the yard. Youngsters were sobbing. Parents were frantically running and calling out for their sons and daughters. Teachers were trying to maintain order. It was pandemonium.

The little ones formed a circle around me and wouldn't let go of one another's hands. I needed to reassure them.

"Let us stay right where we are, and this way your parents will find you."

They nodded their heads solemnly and looked about at the

surrounding confusion. Rodney was holding onto me tightly, and I saw anxiety in his eyes.

"Don't worry, Rodney, your mum will be here."

I had just said this when I heard my name being called frantically, and saw my own mother. She spotted me and ran to me.

"Peter, thank God! But, what happened to you?"

I realized that above the waist I only wore an undershirt which was covered with Rodney's blood. I looked pretty awful.

"Don't worry, Mum, I'm alright." I told her.

"The blood? Your shirt? What happened to this child, and why are these children with you?" She stammered almost incoherently.

"They were---" I was interrupted.

"Sir saved me!" shouted Rodney

"SIR SAVED US!" They all screamed in unison.

Before I could continue any further David and Doreen were rushing toward me. Doe's eyes were very red, and David's nose was running. Anyone looking at them would have suspected they had been crying. Doe threw her arms around me, and in the process squashed poor little Rodney who let out a yelp. David stood a few feet away and kept wiping his nose with the back of his hand. Doe stepped back, and in a very shaky voice started to speak.

"When we got into the shelter you weren't there. No one knew where you were. We thought you had stayed in the school, and it was bombed. Peter, we all thought you were---"

She never finished this last statement because she began sobbing. David who had been staring at his shoes, walked up to me, hit me on my back, slowly turned away, and quietly sniffled. My classmates had been thinking the worst the entire time I was singing and playing with my nursery group. David composed himself and his voice rose above all others.

"BLIMEY, *MATE*, DON'T YOU EVER DO THAT AGAIN TO ME!"

My mother took Rodney from me so that I could explain what had occurred to my friends, but even that had to wait.

Chapter Fifteen

Parents swarmed around us. Everyone was either crying or laughing. Teachers joined us and asked what seemed like hundreds of questions. The children shouted and talked all at once. Nothing anyone was saying made any sense.

Feeling superior to the other children, since he had been wounded, Rodney cried out exuberantly.

"LISTEN, LISTEN TO ME EVERYONE! I'LL TELL YOU WHAT HAPPENED!"

Rodney was in his glory. Being up in my mother's arms he had an advantage over the other children on the ground below him. All eyes were riveted on him.

"Our teacher took sick and had to leave us. She promised she would be back in a few minutes, and she told us to color in our books. But she didn't come back, and the sirens blared, and we didn't know what to do."

Jenny skipped up to my mother, and pulled on her *cardigan*.

"Can I talk now, Missus, please?"

My mother whispered in Rodney's ear, and he answered for my mother.

"You can tell a little bit now, Jenny, but remember it's my story."

Everyone now turned their attention to Jenny.

"I was really scared. I hid under teacher's desk. Ian tried to get me out. I wouldn't get out, then Sir came."

When Jenny pointed at me, a murmur rose from the crowd, so I was about to explain, but she continued without stopping for air.

"Sir spoke nice to me, and I came out, and he put me on his shoulders, and Sir told us to be a centipede, and he took us to the shelter,

115

and he tore off his shirt, and Rodney's blood was all over, and Rodney didn't die, and we were all saved by Sir."

Rodney stared at Jenny in disbelief. She had stolen his thunder. Personally, I thought that Jenny's speech explained everything quite well, but parents and teachers wanted to hear my side.

After what seemed like forever, all questions were answered, and every child recovered. Rodney was reunited with his mother and father who could not thank me enough for what I had done for their little son. Lucy's mother told me she was shocked I had been able to get her daughter into the shelter. Apparently during the nightly attacks, mother and child had been taking cover under a table in the parlor rather than go into the Anderson shelter with the rest of the family. Lucy beamed when I winked at her, after all we had shared the same fears. David's and Doe's mums were busy talking to my mother as we finally all headed home, and behind us the remains of the school smoldered.

Doe hooked her arm through mine, and David took his place on my other side. Our mothers walked behind us yet we could hear their soft chatting. David kept hitting me on the back, while simultaneously letting out a deep breath. Meanwhile, Doe was unusually quiet, but every now and then looked up at me, and sighed. We three were together again and that was all that mattered.

When we came to Doe's street, she hugged me, reached up, and kissed me on the cheek. At the same time, she whispered in my ear.

"You're my favorite pal, Peter, don't ever forget that."

There was no time to respond, because she trotted off with her mother. David who had been watching all this started laughing.

"Maybe you should scare her more often so you can get kissed."

"Real funny, David," I happily answered.

Both our mothers had walked on ahead, and now were at the end of David's road. Whatever they were talking about was obviously very serious, because both their faces were deep in thought. David started into his road. He stopped, coughed, and in a quivering voice said,

"I was afraid for you, Peter."

"I know, David."

He nodded, waved goodbye, and very slowly continued down the street. Our mums kept talking, so I decided not to learn what it was all about. Mum would tell me eventually.

At home the gate was open so Toffee ran out the garden to meet me with her usual greeting, but before she could begin running around me I picked her up, rubbed her ears, and held her close.

"My Toffee! I was worried about you, but you don't look any the worse for today's attack."

The spaniel licked my face, wiggled out of my arms, and ran to my mother who had entered the garden just as my father and sister came rushing out the back door. Daddy looked distraught, Tillie was crying, but when they saw me they both shouted riotously. My father held me so tightly I couldn't breathe while Tillie danced around us. Finally, Daddy let me go,

"We both got home just a few minutes ago," Tillie said.

"The A.R.P. warden just left, when he told us the school had been bombed, we didn't know what to think. We assumed you had gone to the school, Margaret, and we were hurrying to meet you there. Peter, my boy, thank heaven you are safe," my father said.

"What happened? Is it true the school has been totally demolished? Are all the students alright? Where were you when they attacked?" Tillie rambled on.

"There is a lot to tell. Peter has quite a tale for you both. He is a true hero. He saved an entire nursery class today," Mum announced.

My father looked at me in amazement, and Tillie for once was speechless.

"He'll tell you all about it over tea, but first, Peter, go wash up, and change into some clean clothes," Mum said being ever practical.

My undershirt and uniform pants were covered in blood and dirt. My face was streaked with soot and my hair was standing up on end. I looked a sight. No wonder everyone was shocked when they first saw me. I looked as though I had been fighting the war single handed.

During tea time, I told my entire story. I did not leave out anything, including my own fears and revelations. No one interrupted me, and it wasn't until I had finished that Daddy raised his head from his hands and looked intently at me.

"Peter, I am very proud of you. You took on a great responsibility when you brought those children into the shelter. You're a very brave young man!"

"Thanks, Daddy." His words choked me up.

He continued looking at me very seriously and spoke again.

"Events today have changed many things for us all."

"Yes, I have proved that I can stay in a shelter, so you won't send me north?"

"You have proven your courage, but it does not change my opinion that you are safer away from London," Daddy said this, shook his head, and continued talking.

"The war has extended to all the countries from which I import, so it's impossible to obtain citrus fruits. The other night's *Blitz* seriously damaged our warehouse. I don't intend to repair it, because I am certain it will only be hit again. I have locked up the office, and will not be returning."

This news shocked me. I had never really thought how the war was affecting Daddy's business. How could I have been so thoughtless? I was only concerned about myself and my silly problems.

"On top of all of this, we received a letter yesterday from our tenants who for the past two years have been renting our cottage near Oxford. They have the opportunity to move to Scotland, and are leaving next month. The timing is not good. We could have used that money."

"Daddy, what will we do?" I stammered.

"I'll figure something out," Daddy assured me, but both my parents looked worried.

"Is that the house in Watlington?" I asked as my mind had started working.

"Yes, why do you ask?"

"Well, with you closing your business, there really isn't any reason for us to stay in London."

I had gotten my parents attention, so I continued.

"We could shut this house up and go live in Watlington. This way we can all be together. Tillie won't have to find a flat, I won't have to go to Auntie Nan's, and Toffee can stay with us!"

Mum, Dad and Tillie looked at one another. Slowly a smile spread across each of their faces.

"What a brilliant idea!" Tillie shouted.

"Yes, absolutely brilliant. The bombings have become too frequent here. We shall lock up this house, and hope for the best. With so many young men going off to war, I shouldn't have any problem obtaining a job in Oxford. I might even volunteer for the *Home Guard.* Margaret, what do you think?"

"I think I must telegraph Nan, and tell her to disregard your previous telegram. I'll write to her and give her all the information once we settle in."

"I'm not going north! Hooray!"

"Now you won't have to stand up to that bully, Colin," Mum said ever so slyly.

"You knew about Colin? However, did you know about him?"

"Well your father and I knew that it wasn't Nan nor the farm that you didn't like. We remembered that Nan had written us about a London boy who had arrived in Carlisle with you. She mentioned that he seemed to terrorize you at every turn you took. Something about hiding the donkey and her cart, if I recall."

My mouth dropped. Auntie Nan was not as oblivious as I had thought. She had been aware of everything that was going on. I was stunned, and Tillie took this opportunity to chime in.

"Feeling a tiny bit silly, brother? Did you really think you could hide things from Auntie Nan? She even knew when I had a crush on the post-man, and I was only eleven at the time!"

We all had a good laugh over that one, and then I realized something. Watlington wasn't that far from Princes Risborough where Doe was going. This was fabulous, but then I remembered yet another thing. David was going to be shipped off to Ireland. I suddenly stopped laughing, and my face must have told how I felt.

"Peter, now what is wrong?" Daddy questioned me.

"Well, I was just thinking that Doe is going off to Princes Risborough to stay with her grandmother. We'll be rather near to Risborough, and

I'll be able to see her quite often, but David is being sent to his sister's in Ireland. Who knows when he'll come back."

"Ah yes, that is a problem. Ireland is much farther away than Princes Risborough," Mummy said.

"Mum, Dad, maybe, but only if it's okay with you, we could ask David's parents if he could join us, rather than go off to Ireland? I don't mind us sharing the same room."

While I suggested this, I kept my fingers crossed behind my back. My mother answered first.

"I don't see why not. It's a very good suggestion. David's mother is quite concerned about sending him to Ireland. The crossing has become very dangerous. Ships have been bombed while sailing over."

Dad placed his hand on my shoulder and I waited nervously for his decision.

"Peter, your friend is indeed welcome. Why don't you take a ride over, and tell him what you have solved for all of us?"

I'm not much for kissing my parents, but this was one time I made an exception. I kissed Mum on her cheek, and Dad on his forehead. I gave Tillie a big hug and ran out the back. I carted my bike from the shed, jumped on, and cycled at top speed to David's. Earlier this morning I had felt nothing would ever make me happy again, how wrong I had been!

All sorts of things rushed into my mind as I sped on. Would I go to school in Oxford or Watlington? When would we leave? Were we hiring a *lorry* to transport all our belongings? Things were really exciting.

The war would continue, the Nazis would still be flying over London, and trying to conquer all of Europe, but for the moment, I had nothing to fear!

This called for a song. "Old MacDonald had a farm, E-I-E-I-O".

Epilogue

Dearest Auntie Nan,

What a super birthday gift! Thank you so much. Your painting of the cottage here in Watlington, is amazing, I hung it over my bed.

David likes to lie on his bed and look at it before falling off to sleep. He says it gives him good dreams.

I was very surprised by the news you wrote about Colin. I always thought there was something amiss with him. I remember how sometimes he looked sad and far away from everything. It all makes sense now that we know his father took the strap to him whenever the man got drunk. No wonder Colin is happier on his grandfather's farm and has refused to return to London. He's a strong bloke and should make a good farmer. Don't you think?

Life here outside of Oxford is very nice. David and I attend school and have met several decent fellows. We even joined a cricket team. We get to see Doe quite often. It's not such a distance to cycle from Princes Risborough to Watlington

Guess what? Mum is working with Madame Gina and Jillie! The shop is bustling and Mum loves it.

Daddy has joined the Home Guard. This week he started his new job at Christ College. I've not seen Daddy so happy in a long time.

How is Mercury? Have you entered any more competitions? Is Daffodil behaving? Have you named the bunnies? Oh! What a lot of questions I have for you.

Please write soon. Thank you again for the painting. All my love, your nephew, Peter

P.S. I wonder if Colin was bullying me just to get my attention? Did he want to make friends and had no idea how to go about it? Perhaps one day we'll have the answer to my questions.

Glossary

ack-acks—antiaircraft guns

Air Raid Precaution Warden (A.R.P.) – patrolled the streets during and after blackouts

barmy-idiotic

barrage balloon-a large balloon tethered with metal cables, used to defend against low-level attack by aircraft by damaging the aircraft on collision with the cables, or at least making the attackers approach more difficult.

batty-crazy

billeted—accommodated, boarded

biscuit—cookie

blimey–Wow!

Blitz–a fast violent military attack

Blitzkrieg–German, meaning lightning war, military attack

bloke–guy

Bobby–English policeman

bonnet–hood of car

boot–trunk of car

Boxing Day–December 26th, legal holiday in Great Britain when friends and family visit each other and exchange gifts. Arrived at its name from when the churches opened their poor boxes on December 26th and gave the contents to the poor.

bums–bottoms, buttocks

cardigan–a sweater which buttons up the front

Cockney–Londoners from the East End; a dialect unique to the East End Londoners

crackers-crazy

cricket–an outdoor ball game

daft–crazy

digs–rental apartment

Dunkirk-an evacuation of over 300,000 Allied troops occurred off the beaches of Dunkirk, France, from May 27 through June 4, 1940, by sea going vessels of all sizes including fishing boats, pleasure cruisers, commercial vessels, ferries, and military ships.

fells–barren hills

fortnight–two weeks

goose step–stiff manner of marching

hamper–a basket used for picnics

Heinkel 111–Nazi bomber

Home Guard-was a defense organization of the British Army, composed of approximately 1.5 million local volunteers who were either too old, or too young for military service.

incendiary bomb–bomb that erupts into fire

kippers-smoked herring

lino-linoleum

lorry-truck

Luftwaffe–Nazi air force

marrow–vegetable, squash

mate–best friend

Messerschmitt–Nazi fighter plane

nécessaire–French for-necessary

oil cloth–cotton fabric coated one side with mixture of vegetable oils, pigments and clay making it water proof

petrol–gasoline

pram–baby or doll carriage

Put' n Take–game played for money involving a top like spinner

R.A.F.-(British) Royal Air Force

Right-o - Okay

scone–comparable to a biscuit in the USA

Selfridge–department store in London

shilling–a British silver coin worth 12 pence (no longer in circulation)

sixpence–a British silver coin worth six pennies (no longer in circulation)

Snakes and Ladders–board game in United States called Chutes and Ladders

spanner–hand tool used to tighten nuts and bolts

Spitfire – British fighter plane

stone–measure of weight equaling approximately 14 pounds

sweets-candies

tartan–a plaid design specific for each Scottish clan

torch–flash light

trap-mouth

Underground–the London subway system

valise–luggage, suitcase

W.C.–wash closet, bathroom

wellingtons–high rubber waterproof boots going up to the knees

wireless–radio

Author's Notes

On **September 1, 1939** Nazi Germany invaded Poland. Two days following this act of aggression Great Britain's Prime Minister, Neville Chamberlain, on Sunday, September 3rd at 11:15AM announced "…this country is at war with Germany…" Immediately after, at 11:27AM, the wail of the air raid sounded. The "howl of the banshee" was a false alarm, but became a sound which the inhabitants of London would become all too familiar.

On **August 1, 1939** "Operation Pied Piper" was established. On the first four days of September alone, an estimated three million people, the majority children of all ages, were evacuated from London and other cities believed to be targeted by the Nazis. Children were sent to the country and *billeted* with strangers. Prior to September 1940 many children were sent to British commonwealths. On **September 23, 1940,** a ship en route to Canada with ninety children aboard was torpedoed. Eighty-three children were killed, and the practice of sending children overseas came to a halt immediately. While the majority of *billeted* children had memorable experiences with the people who put them up, reports of child abuse surfaced. During the "Phony War", so named because the Nazis attacks were of little consequence following Britain's declaration of war, many parents brought their children home back to the cities.

In May of 1940 Prime Minister Chamberlain resigned, and Winston Churchill was appointed Prime Minister. Churchill addressed the British people assuring them victory would be attained "…at all costs…in spite of all terror." His eloquence made him a great inspiration to the embattled British. Perhaps one of his greatest speeches to the British was that he had "…nothing to offer, but blood, toil, tears and sweat."

At 4:00PM on **September 7, 1940** the sky over London darkened when a reported 348 German bombers, and 617 fighter planes flew in a twenty-mile-wide block formation toward the city. The Nazis Blitzkrieg had begun and would continue until May 10, 1941. Weather permitting, the Nazis planes attacked London nightly and on occasion during the day. For a duration of seventy-six consecutive nights the residents of London had little sleep with one exception, when a heavy fog prevented the Nazis pilots to fly from occupied France to England.

It was estimated that over 170,000 people sought safety in the *Underground* system of London, and others found shelter at home in Anderson shelters, and even under tables, beds and stairs. During those months, more than 29,000 civilians were killed in London alone, and an estimated 25,000 people were injured. May 10, 1941 the last night of the Blitz, proved to be the most catastrophic night when greater than 3,000 Londoners were killed and more than 2000 fires erupted over 700 acres of London.

Over one million homes and businesses were either destroyed or damaged during the Blitz in London. Buckingham Palace, as well as Westminster Abbey, architect Sir Christopher Wren's St. Paul's Cathedral, and the Houses of Parliament were bombed, as were many other countless historic buildings. In September 1940, early on during the Blitz, the South Hallsville School received a direct hit reducing the school to rubble. The school was being used as a shelter, and casualty rates were a source of extreme skepticism for years. Even *Underground* stations which served as shelters were not spared. On October 14, 1940, a bomb fell above Baltham Tube Station. A London bus crashed into the resulting crater and the platform below collapsed. Water from demolished sewer pipes flooded the station and approximately sixty-four people were killed and many more injured. On December 29, 1940, the historic Greyfriar's Christ Church burned to the ground. Today its ruins remain a tourist attraction. The House of Commons burned down on May 10, 1941.

Despite London's devastation, the proud people of this historic city were never brought to their knees as Hitler had envisioned. As the days of the Blitz dragged on Londoners became stronger in their conviction that Great Britain would withstand the onslaught and win the war against the Nazi regime. During the Blitz, Winston Churchill stated Hitler knew little of the "...spirit of the British nation or the tough fiber of the Londoners..." Many historians believe it was this fortitude Churchill referred to that resulted in Hitler's decision to halt the bombing and the invasion of England.

Today the carnage of the London Blitz is commemorated throughout the city, in the form of countless Memorial Plaques giving tribute to the thousands who lost their lives, thus telling their stories for generations to follow.

Bibliography

Publications

Gaskin, Margaret. <u>BLITZ, The Story of December 29, 1940</u>. Orlando, FLA: Harcourt, Inc.2005.

Grolier Educational. <u>Battle of Britain</u>. Danbury, CT: Grolier Publishing Company, Inc. 1995.

Harris, Clive. <u>Walking the London Blitz</u>. Barnsley, South Yorkshire: Pen & Sword Books Ltd. 2003.

McGowen, Tom. <u>Air Raid! The Bombing Campaigns of WWII</u>. Buffalo, NY: Twenty-first Century Books, 2001.

Morrow, Edward R. <u>This Is London</u>. New York, NY: Schocken Books. 1941.

Sheehan, Sean. <u>WWII: The Allied Victory The World Wars</u>. Austin, TX: Raintree, Steck-Vaughn Publishers. 2001.

Stansky, Peter. <u>The 1st Day of the Blitz: September 7, 1940</u>. New Haven, CT: Yale University Press. 2007.

Townsend, Peter. <u>Duel of Eagles</u>. New York, NY: Simon and Schuster.1971.

Westall, Robert. <u>Children of the Blitz, Memories of Wartime Childhood</u>. New York, NY: Viking Press.1985.

Resources

http:/www.livingmemory.org.uk/images/Homefront_Recall

http:/www.fortuncity.co.uk/meltingpot/oxford

http://www.enWikipedia.org/wiki/TheBlitz

Links

Air Raid Sirens followed by the All Clear (Very good quality recording)

Alternative Anthem of the United Kingdom-"God Save the King" Youtube.com

BBC Archive-www.bbc.co.uk/archive/ww2outbreak

eastlondonshistory.co.uk

Farm animal sounds-Animal-Sounds.org

Knees Up Mother Brown Cockney Rubble

Old MacDonald had a farm | Learn English Kids | British Council

Onward Christian Soldiers-Manchester Citadel Band-Yorkshire Chorus You Tube

The Real Kings Speech King George VI September 3rd 1939 You Tube

Winston Churchill's Most Important Speeches-Telegraph www. telegraph.co.uk

Acknowledgements

To my dear friend, Jenny Cella, thank you for forgoing weekends of frivolity to read and edit my manuscript. I am exceedingly grateful to my cousin, Dr. Donald Marinelli, Professor of Drama & Arts Management (Retired), Carnegie Mellon University, who took time from his hectic life to methodically critique my work while giving me a few bruises along the way.

Without Dr. Paul van Wie, Associate Professor of History and Political Science, Molloy College, Rockville Centre, NY, *Peter and the Blitz* would not have been my dream come true. I am deeply indebted to him for his enthusiasm and guidance.

Special thanks to my brother, Pascal, who emotionally supported me in this endeavor, and I especially thank my husband, Joseph, who many evenings was satisfied with a quick omelet for dinner while I sat in front of my computer.

Artist

Harriet Carotenuto is an artist, teacher and lecturer whose career as an art teacher has extended from kindergarten through high school. She earned a Master of Fine Arts from City University of New York, NY, a Bachelor of Science in Art Education from Pratt Institute, Brooklyn, NY and a Certificate in Botanical Illustration from the NY Botanic Garden. Her paintings have been internationally exhibited, and has received numerous awards. Harriet is a founding member of the American Society of Botanical Artists. She serves on the Boards of the Art League of Nassau County, NY, and The Friends of the Hempstead Plains at Nassau Community College, NY.